About the author

Kathryn is a single mum of two boys, originally from Sheffield, South Yorkshire, but now lives in a small town in Lancashire. As well as writing, Kathryn loves everything creative, especially cross stitching; she owns a small arts and crafts business which she runs from the local indoor market. She loves to watch sports including Formula One and football, which her eldest son plays. She also loves to travel and explore cultural places; she lived in Greece for five years and also worked in the US for a summer season.

PUTTING EVERYTHING ON THE LINE

Kathryn Pana

PUTTING EVERYTHING ON THE LINE

Vanguard Press

VANGUARD PAPERBACK

A CIP catalogue record for this title is
available from the British Library.

ISBN 978 1 784655 15 0

*Vanguard Press is an imprint of
Pegasus Elliot MacKenzie Publishers Ltd.*
www.pegasuspublishers.com

First Published in 2019

**Vanguard Press
Sheraton House, Castle Park
Cambridge, England**

Printed & Bound in Great Britain

Dedication

For my boys, who are my world.

For my friends, who have supported my journey.

For Elly, who has been an inspiration.

Prologue

Six Years Earlier

It was a quiet day for the alpha team in the New York SWAT unit. Sergeant Will Falco and his team were training down on the indoor range. Will had only had the team for two years and he had put together the best shooters in the unit. His oldest and best friend, Tom Hargreaves, had just joined him on Team Alpha after some negotiation with the captain. Will had found being a team leader harder than he expected and he needed some support.

Some of his team were new to SWAT so they needed training. Will wanted his team to keep their Alpha status and perfect all their skills.

'Sergeant, is that better?' asked Turner, his newest member.

'Yeah, better than before but you still have a couple of strays,' Will said, looking at the target.

Will had always been a near perfect shot –
many said it was a gift, a natural talent. He was
one of the youngest to ever join the unit. He
was pushed to take his Sergeant's exam and to
lead his own team before he was thirty.

As they were setting up their new targets,
their beepers went.

'OK, let's go, guys,' Will said, and they all
followed him out to the truck, collecting their
weapons as they went.

***

They arrived at a police cordon. It was a quiet
street and there wasn't any big stores, just small
businesses and residential properties. Will got
out and went over to the officer in charge as the
truck was waved through the tape and stopped.
They had a brief conversation about the
situation while his team got out and got suited
up. Will was looking around at the surrounding
buildings as he went back to his team, he
started getting ready as he briefed them.

'OK, we have a group of armed assailants in
a small jewellery store down here on the right-
hand side of the road. Now me and Hargreaves
will be on the roof exactly opposite. The

building is a perfect height, so we should get a good view of the inside and what's going on in there. Turner and Harvey, I want you on this building. You need to look out for any escape routes and vehicles and be ready to stop those on command. Barker and O'Neill, I need you two down on the ground to cover the officers and residents. If this goes south, I need you to be on your game. Now they have several hostages, there is the owner and staff, the rest are customers. We need to be at our best with this one. There are a lot of lives on the line here.'

They all got their appropriate rifles from the truck and headed to their positions as quickly as they could.

'So, what do you have planned for your birthday? Are you heading to your parents at all?' Tom asked Will as they headed off to their position.

'Yeah, probably, but we will be going out for some beers one night, too.'

'What, no date with your lovely other? Or is she going to your parents with you?'

'No, she is having some issues with my mum, so she is staying away.'

They started heading up the stairs to the roof.

'Not like your parents? We are talking about the same people, aren't we? The lovely couple that have treated me so amazing since we were kids. The ones who get me a Christmas and birthday present every year without fail and got me an awesome wedding present. Why does she not like them? I wish they were my parents.'

'Well, you aren't my fiancée. They are insisting on a pre-nup and said there won't be a wedding without one. She has gone crazy about it, saying if I make her sign it then I don't trust her, but my parents are saying if she doesn't sign it, then she is just after the money and will probably disappear within the first year.' He opened the door to the roof. 'I really don't know what to do.'

They walked slowly to the edge and got their rifles ready. The wall around the edge provided perfect cover while they did this. So many buildings in New York had these and because the roof was so accessible, they were always useful for the SWAT teams on sniper detail.

Tom was ready and looked through his scope to get focussed and aimed in on the store. He froze and moved away from the scope.

Will looked at him, puzzled.

'What's up? You look like you've seen a ghost.'

'They have lined the hostages along the window so we can't see in or get a clean shot, and that's not all,' he paused, not knowing how to say the words he needed to. 'Your parents are in there.'

Will looked through his scope and saw them stood in the window with the other hostages. His mother looked so frightened.

'What the hell? I can't believe this. What are they even doing here? They don't shop in this area. Why today?'

'Will, do you want to step back? I can take over.'

'No.' He walked up and down. 'No, you can't. No one knows that they are my parents, remember?'

'Will, what are you going to do? You can't pretend they aren't down there, neither of us can.'

'I have to, so I can get them out alive.' He paused for a moment. 'Alpha Team are in position,' he said on the radio.

'Do you have a clear shot, Alpha Team?'

'Negative, they have put the hostages in the window. If we can draw them out, we will though.'

'We are on the phone with them now, stand by.'

Will looked at the window, trying to work out how he was going to get through this and get his parents out alive.

***

Twenty minutes past and still no movement.

'Alpha Team, we have a standoff with those inside. The order is if you can get a clear shot, then you are to take it.'

'Alpha Team, received that.'

'This is not good,' Tom said. 'These never end good. What now?'

'We shoot the bastards one by one and get as many hostages out as possible.'

'Hey, something's happening. One of the hostages has moved,' Tom exclaimed.

'Yeah, I see it. I can see one of the assailants. He has a gun on a hostage. I'm taking the shot.'

Will fired. The window broke, the assailant, shot dead, fell, hanging out of the window. Suddenly, the hostages were dragged from the windows and two more gunmen came to the windows, shooting at the police down on street level.

'One each,' Will said to Tom, while still looking through his scope.

'Yeah, I got left,' Tom answered.

'1... 2... 3.'

Two shots rang out and the assailants were down. A car came speeding round the corner and stopped right outside the store.

'Harvey, he's yours,' Will said on the radio.

One shot sounded, the driver was down. Will was looking through his scope, searching for anyone else in the store but he couldn't see anyone at all. He knew there had to be another assailant or the hostages would have come out.

Suddenly, he heard six shots coming from inside the store. Will looked over at Tom, his heart pounding. He looked back and the store door opened. Will could see his dad, there was another man behind him. He followed them as they moved down the street in desperate hope that he would show himself, that he could get him before he killed his dad. This guy was good though – not ever enough of him for long enough. He knew what he was doing. Then they disappeared round the corner.

Police slowly started to follow. Will had started getting ready to move and then he heard another shot, he fell to the floor.

Tom looked down at the street, police had entered the store and were heading off round the corner. Officers being ordered in all directions, then it came over the radio.

'All hostages are down, the remaining assailant has gone.'

Will felt his heart pounding. He took off his helmet and took his earpiece out. He put his head in his hands. Tears rolled down his face.

Tom paced in disbelief, shaking his head.

'Will, we have to go. You can't stay here.'

'I know,' he answered.

Tom pulled him up, they collected their things and started walking slowly towards the door. Will stopped for a moment and looked at Tom.

'I can't believe he just did that.' He paused and looked back to the edge of the roof, then back at Tom. 'He just shot them all, for what?

He didn't need to do that. He could have negotiated his way out. We didn't have a choice, did we?' Almost questioning what he himself had done in the line of duty.

'No, he didn't have to, but you know some guys are crazy, they don't have normal thoughts. I can't even imagine what you are going through right now or why this happened, but you need to go down there and do your job right now. Your parents did everything to protect you and no one down there knows who they are. You OK to do this?'

'No, but you're right, we need to move.'

He opened the door and walked in silence down the stairs and out onto the street. Will started walking towards the store.

Tom put his arm up to stop him and whispered, 'You don't want to see her like that.'

Will nodded and headed to the truck, all the team were there waiting, stunned in silence.

Just as Will and Tom were putting their stuff away, Will's phone rang. His mum's picture flashed up on the screen.

He signalled to Tom and they moved away from the truck.

'Hello?' he answered.

'William, I presume?' came the reply.

'Yeah, who is this?'

'That's not important…' Just then, a siren went by and he heard it on the phone. Will realised he was close by, but he heard it, too.

'You are here, William, you know,' he paused with a chuckle. 'You are a policeman, aren't you? And you just had the privilege of watching me kill your mother and father. Wait, it gets better. You are SWAT. You are the reason I had to kill them.'

Will spun round looking for him but he didn't even know what he looked like.

'Well, come and get me. That's if you can find me,' and he hung up.

Will walked back to the truck.

'Let's go,' he said to the team, then he pulled Tom to the back of the truck. 'He is still watching and he knows who I am.'

'Shit,' Tom responded. 'What now?'

'I find and kill the bastard,' Will said. 'But first I need to get back and speak to the captain to get their identity covered up before people start putting things together. I can't go after this guy or run this team if it comes out who I am.'

Five Years Earlier

Kathy was home preparing dinner when Tony walked in after his shift. For once they had both been on days, and so Kathy had rushed home to prepare his dinner, he had started to get over the fact she was working for the Chicago police department, but she wasn't sure how he would take her latest news so she had made his favourite in hope it would soften him up before telling him. For her, it was a definite step up and she wouldn't be at ground level any more, it did mean more money too, though not that much so it wasn't really a selling point. She knew he had being making hints of her leaving after they got married and had suggested having children several times of late. She, however, wanted to see what she could achieve professionally first though.

'Hi, Hun,' she said, smiling.

'Hi, baby,' he replied before kissing her.

'Good day?' she asked.

'Yeah, not too much going on today thankfully. You?'

'I had an amazing day actually.' She started serving dinner.

Tony was getting in the way, picking off the plates before she was done.

'Why, what happened?'

'Well, my sergeant pulled me in his office. I thought I had done something wrong at first, because that's why he usually does that, but he said my record was exemplary and my scores on the range are one of the best from my precinct. So, they want me to move onto the SWAT unit.'

'Are you serious?' he asked sternly.

'Yeah, why?'

'You want to put yourself in more danger than you do now?'

'Says you that goes into burning buildings most days of the week.'

'That's different and you know it is.' He paused and held her shoulders, looking into her eyes. 'You know I want kids and I want you to leave the force as soon as we get married, so why do this?'

She shrugged him off and walked to the other end of the kitchen.

'Because I want to, because I am good enough and I want to be the best police officer I can be. This opportunity is rare for female officers, I can't and I won't turn this down.'

Tony headed towards the door collecting his coat en-route.

'Where are you going? What about dinner?'

'Out.' He opened the door. 'I lost my appetite.' He left, slamming the door.

***

She was in bed when he came home but she couldn't sleep, it was probably a good thing she wasn't on shift tomorrow. She could hear him in the kitchen, he was most likely hungry after walking out on dinner. A short time later, she could hear him in the bathroom and then there was complete silence. He didn't come to bed, he must have gone into the spare room or something. She sighed as she laid in the dark, she began thinking about the future. Why could he not see that she loved her job and wanted to be more? To achieve something and the fact that she was good at this was the reason that she needed to see what she could do and where this would take her. It took her a while to fall asleep but when she did, she slept better than she had in weeks.

The next day when Kathy woke, the house was quiet. She got up and went into the kitchen and put on some coffee, she looked in the living room, Tony wasn't there. She went and looked outside, his car was gone. She took a shower and as she was coming back into the kitchen for her coffee, the phone rang.

'Hello?' she answered.

'Kathy, Tony called last night, completely distraught, something about you joining the SWAT unit. Now is this true?'

'Hi Mum, yeah it's true. The sergeant wants me to take the exams. He thinks I have a good chance at passing.'

'Well I don't think so, young lady. I want grandchildren sometime soon and this is no way to go about it.'

'There is plenty of time for that, Mum, and I do have to pass first. It is one of the hardest units to get into.'

'Pass or not, this whole police thing has gone far enough and you should stop playing games and do what is right.'

'What is right for who? You? Tony?' Kathy paused to catch her breath, she was so angry. He had gone behind her back to her parents. 'You don't care what I want for my life as long as it suits you and Tony. I love my job and I am honoured to be asked to try out for SWAT, and you, quite frankly, don't have to like it, Mum, because it is my decision.'

'So, that's it? You will throw your whole future away for this?'

'I am making my future, Mum, by doing this.' Kathy replied and then she hung up; she couldn't take any more. She was so tired of being told what she should be doing and what was best for her. She was going to do this and she would try her very best to make it work with Tony because she did love him, but if he couldn't handle this, then she would have to make a choice and she knew deep down what that would be.

Three Years Earlier

'Kathy, I have been thinking,' Tony shouted as he came in. 'We should rent out your grandmother's house, save for the wedding, take a holiday. We could take your parents away, they said they would love to go back to Florida.'

Just then, Kathy came from the bedroom with two suitcases. He looked at her questioningly.

'Are you going somewhere?'

'Yes, I am going to New York,' she replied.

'To sort the house out? How long will you be gone for? Because you never mentioned it to me or your mum.'

'No, not to sort the house out. I am going to stay there for a while and decide what I want. I can't do that here with you and my mum constantly deciding what is best for me without thinking about what I want.' She started walking towards the door.

'What do you mean?'

'Us. I don't know if we have a future, because you have never supported me in anything and I am tired of it, so I am going to New York to stay in my house and I will work out what I am going to do next.'

'Should we not be doing that together? Are you prepared to throw everything away? Our whole relationship? For what? Because I don't like you being a police officer?'

'Don't like? That's an understatement. You have expected me to quit since the day I joined the force. I am not prepared to sacrifice what I have built and that part of my life and who I am.' She paused at the door. 'I have been given a transfer to the New York SWAT team and if it suits me, then I will stay. I am really sorry,

Tony, but if you can't support my dream, then I have to find someone who will,' and with that she left.

***

When she arrived in New York, she unpacked and got settled in her new home. She had stayed there many times before but it was strange now her grandmother had gone. She had decided she was going to use her grandmother's old furniture until she could afford new, most of it was still in good condition except for the bed, so she would sleep in her old room for now till she could get a new one and redecorate. Her phone flashed, her mother was calling again, she had had seventeen missed calls since she left but she still wasn't ready to have that conversation.

After unpacking she had a drive round the area locating stores and facilities, things hadn't changed much since she was last there, but her needs were different now it was her home. She then stopped by the SWAT unit, which was attached to one of the central districts. She had paperwork to fill in and uniform to collect. She was starting in just two days and had so much to do. She was shown upstairs, there was two teams sat at desks talking and typing, she wondered if one of them was her new team. They looked up as she walked in.

Captain Bridge was waiting for her at the far side, at the door to his office, she followed him inside and he shut the door.

'Officer Hill, welcome to NYPD SWAT. Now I have glowing references for Chicago. Seems they were very sorry to lose you and so I have assigned you to Sergeant Falco's team. He runs the Alpha Team which is our designated sniper team.'

'What? Really?' she responded, shocked.

'If you don't think you can handle that I can try and rearrange...?'

'No, it's fine, honestly, Captain.'

There was a lot of noise coming from the unit office, Captain Bridge got up and opened his door and shouted, 'Sergeant Falco, get in here.'

Kathy got a sudden feeling of nervous energy coursing through her. This was a big test for her, the transfer at Chicago was easy as she knew them but to be put in the Alpha Team was huge pressure and she hoped she could handle this. A tall dark-haired man walked in, he didn't acknowledge her at first.

'Captain, it was a clean shoot. That guy was not going to let go of that girl and I had no choice, I swear.'

'Sergeant, for once you are not here to be reprimanded. I want you to meet the newest member of your team. Officer Hill, this is Sergeant Falco.'

She stood and shook his hand and he surveyed her.

'You had better be good, because you won't last long here if you're not,' he said bluntly.

'Sergeant, play nice. She starts on Wednesday so get her uniform and weapons sorted today. Tomorrow, if you like, you can get her down on the range before duty Wednesday.' He looked at Kathy. 'Officer Hill, I will see you then and good luck.'

Kathy followed Will, wondering what the Captain had meant; they headed towards the door and then he stopped in front of another officer.

'Tom, this is our new recruit from Chicago. Show her around, sort uniform and weapons.' He looked at Kathy. 'What's your favourite colour?'

'Purple,' she answered, puzzled.

'OK, that's your call sign.' He paused. 'Now, be here at nine a.m., and I don't accept lateness for any reason. We will go on the range and see if you are good enough to sit at these desks, because believe me, most aren't.'

With that he walked off to a small office next to the Captain's and shut the door behind him.

'Is he always like that?' Kathy asked.

'Yes, till he trusts you,' Tom answered. 'Come on, I will show you around and get you sorted.'

Chapter One

It was a beautiful spring day, not a cloud in the sky and it was already bright blue with the sun shining brightly. It was already warm and the smell of the spring blossom filled the air. There were already people on their way to work or walking dogs.

Kathy Hill was going to be late for work. She came running out of her door, dropped her keys, ran down the steps, dropped her keys again then managed to get in her car. Well she believed it had once been a car but she really wasn't sure when, as now it was all rust and dents and you could barely see it had once been blue. She turned the key in the ignition and nothing. She was running late after sleeping through her alarm, which she had never done before, but last night she had struggled to get to sleep. When she woke, there was a mad dash to get ready and had to skip breakfast and have a coffee on the go. She tried again but all she got was a splutter. Her old car was on its last legs but she couldn't even dream of affording a newer one, not just yet anyway but she was hoping that soon that would change, she couldn't keep risking being late.

'Come on. Start you damn thing. Don't do this to me, not today. COME ON.'

She hit the steering wheel in frustration, people walking past looked at her suspiciously, she smiled at them then screamed in frustration. Then she took a deep breath and tried again. This time the engine came to life.

'Yes,' she shouted. 'Knew you could do it.'

Kathy was an NYPD officer and today was one of the most important days of her career so far. Three years ago, she had joined the elite New York SWAT unit after serving two years on the same department in Chicago. Not that you would know it to look at her. She was far removed from the male macho type that is usually associated with such a job. She was, in fact, just five-foot-four, petite with fair hair and blue eyes. She was good at her job though and had been recognised as such over the last five years. She had got used to the shock reaction that people gave when they found out what she did, it was usually a look of shock and a

'Really? That's so amazing,' from the person asking, expecting a completely different answer.

The one thing she wasn't prepared for through the last five years though, was the vast difference between Chicago and New York. There seemed to be much higher numbers of gun crimes, or maybe they just had more call outs here, though Chicago was bad enough, but the job in New York was harder, more intense and also more physical. That combined with the fact her team leader was a perfectionist, made the pressure full on every working day. She had never regretted the move though, it had come at a perfect time. She had decided to split from her fiancée after her grandmother passed away, she had been left her a beautiful two story home in the city in her will, so she couldn't resist the idea of a fresh start, and a letter from her grandmother, which she had never shared with anyone, had encouraged her to use it for just that reason. She knew her relationship was coming to an end which made it very difficult to go home to Seattle, as she knew her parents would have refused to let her walk away from her ex, they pretty much treated him like he was their child and not her.

It was still very hard being a woman in a man's world, but she had always enjoyed her job, a fact her family and her ex-fiancée could never understand. She couldn't recall a week since she moved when they hadn't phoned her trying to get her to quit and move back, but she had no intention of doing so, she had even expected one of the family to show up on the door step but as of yet, no one had come to visit her and Tony had not managed to fight to get her back in person. This, though, had made things easier for Kathy as the future was starting to pan out just the way she wanted, so it would only cause more issues than it would solve if they were to appear and try and complicate things.

Traffic was busy as always, she hated the journey to work, passing through Manhattan so close to Times Square was never a pleasure for her, especially at this time of day. She usually got up and set off an hour earlier than she had managed today. It was a good thing that it wasn't so far away.

She had never been late before and this was really not the day to start. Not only were her team involved in a special operation, but it was also the day she would find out exactly what the future would hold for her. She had taken her Sergeant's exam and was waiting to hear if she had passed and ultimately, if the extension of the department would involve her heading her own team. There had been no direct implication that this would be the case if she passed, but she knew a whole new team was being recruited, which meant this was her chance.

She was excited, nervous and thrilled at the thought of what doors could open for her. Then she glanced at the clock.

'No, come on, some of us have to get to work you know,' she shouted.

She had fifteen minutes to get to work and she knew he would be waiting for her.

Chapter Two

The SWAT locker room was small and it needed a coat of paint. There was a locker squeezed in for each member, they weren't very big, and were quite battered, looked they hadn't been replaced for a good few years. They had a separate one to the rest of the Police department which was the only good thing about it. It had a small shower area at one end, but the teams never used it now, especially Kathy, as it was open and there was no privacy. It was, however, always peaceful before the start of shift, most of the officers worked shifts and so it got busy at different times of day, but at eight-thirty a.m., it was quiet.

Sergeant Will Falco was always the first one there. He enjoyed these moments of quiet, it helped him gain composure before he started work. He had been on SWAT for fifteen years and led his own team for eight of those. His methods of training and running his team were not popular and often had received criticism and complaints but they got results and his team were considered 'the best'. His team were the designated sniper team, and if a member didn't match his personal standards, they were side-lined till they were as he wanted. Near perfect. He hadn't always been so hard on his team but after an operation hadn't gone to plan six years earlier, he got tough on his team and even tougher on himself.

So, he pushed his team hard, to strive to be better and encouraged them to improve, he led by example and worked to the limits, both physically and mentally. Some couldn't take it and over the last few years, he had replaced several, but even those who left could never say that it was a negative experience working with him. His job was his life and had been for years. He hadn't been in a serious relationship since his fiancée left him and he always made sure never to mix business with pleasure, though sometimes that was hard.

He opened his locker and started to get ready. Bennett, Palmer and Harvey walked in. Bennett was the youngest at twenty-seven and was only five-foot-six, a fact he never lived down as all the other men towered over him. He was stocky in stature and had brown hair and brown eyes. He was single and had an enthusiastic personality. Palmer was the opposite, he was quiet, which bordered on shyness. He was five-foot-eleven, slim and had blonde hair and blue eyes. He too was single but never had the confidence around women the others had. Harvey was African-American, stood at six-foot-one and was, like Bennett, stocky in stature. He was thirty-one and had been happily married to Serena for the last eight years; Will had attended their wedding as he had worked with Harvey for nearly ten years and when he had taken over the Alpha Team, he made sure that Harvey was there with him.

They went to their lockers and started to get ready.

'Morning, guys,' Will said with a smile. 'Ready for today? Should be an easy one.'

'Ready as always, Sergeant,' Bennett replied.

They began chatting about the events of the weekend when Tom Hargreaves walked in. Tom was the oldest of the team at thirty-eight. He was six-foot-two and an average build. He had dark hair and was the 'go to' guy on the team. Tom had known Will since school, been through it all, joining the force and subsequently SWAT together. He had been around for Will's nearly wedding and the death of his parents. He had also seen the many trophy girlfriends that had graced Will's presence in recent years. He didn't like that part of Will's life but understood and never judged him for it. He himself was married to Lynne and had been for many years now. He had been the only real friend that knew all there was to know about Sergeant Falco. The only one who knew who he really was.

The usual locker room conversations were in full swing when Kathy walked in. She had never been the biggest fan of the 'who was dating who, who was sleeping with who' type talk, but as she was working with five men aged between twenty-seven and thirty-eight, she expected and accepted it for what it was. She found some of it funny and even entertaining and the rest, she had learnt to shut out. But in recent weeks, she was finding that hard especially when it involved Will. The guys never hid their banter or conversations when Kathy was there as they saw her as one of the lads. She was not the newest member, Bennett and Palmer came over a year later, so she had always been around to them and it was usually Bennett that was involved in these conversations.

Will looked at his watch then at her in a very serious manner.

'You only just made it. I suggest you hurry up and get ready, we have a briefing in five minutes.'

Kathy opened her locker and sat down. She looked over at Sergeant Falco, he was half dressed. He had an amazing physique, his body looked like it had been sculptured to perfection. He was tall, six-foot-four, with thick black hair and had the deepest brown eyes; that and his Latin appearance made him easily one of the most attractive men she had ever met. He also had a confidence bordering on arrogance which was strangely but overwhelmingly attractive to her. He was not her type anymore, that's what had attracted her to Tony, and she knew it was not a good idea to even entertain that kind of person again, but she couldn't help it.

Thing was, he hardly acknowledged her any more, except when she did something wrong that is, which fortunately was not that often but something was missing of late and she didn't know why.

'Pull yourself together,' she thought. 'Why would a man like him look at me twice? He dates models not women like me.'

She shook her head and started to get ready. The uniform they wore was completely black. The top was snug fitting to enable it to fit comfortably under the bullet proof vests, both emblazed with the word SWAT front and back. The trousers were also not loose but not overly tight, they couldn't be, but had pockets on the legs, as the whole thing had to be one hundred percent practical for the work they did. The boots were very masculine, but Kathy found them hard wearing and very comfortable. The helmet, she wasn't so keen on but that and the goggles, tinted or clear, were essential for her safety. She wore two hand guns, one on her belt and one on her thigh, and of course her main weapon, which today for a change would not be her sniper rifle. The uniform was not feminine or glamorous, but she loved it.

Will was just about to leave when he glanced over to her. She was just closing her locker and she looked over.

'Wow, she is beautiful,' he thought.

She was not his usual type, but there was just something about her. Maybe it was her bright blue eyes or her amazing smile. He wasn't sure but there was something, and it was something he had to push aside before it got him in trouble. He held her gaze for a brief moment before looking away.

'Come on, let's go,' he said as he left the room.

Chapter Three

The briefing room always reminded Kathy of a school classroom. There was a marker board at the front and three rows of chairs with desks, as it was also used for training purposes, the room was not particularly large but had enough room to be comfortable.

The Captain gave the briefing for all the special operations like the one today, though this one was very different to the usual. Captain Bridge was in his mid-fifties, balding and starting to get a bit large around the waistline. He was five-foot-nine so wasn't really that tall but he had been on the force for thirty-five years in different cities; he had even served on SWAT so he knew what it was like on the ground and had earned his position and the respect of the whole department.

'This operation may sound simple, but we are expecting some kind of offensive at some point,' explained Captain Bridge. 'The witness needs taking to a safe house after threats have been made to her life and that of her children. There are people with her now but you will meet them and move her. Then a team will take over and put her in witness protection.'

'We are not usually asked to move witnesses. Why this one?' asked Tom. 'He is not even in custody yet.'

'Because of the case, because he isn't in custody, and you have been requested to do this,' responded the Captain. 'The man who she has given us information on and is willing to testify against will stop at nothing to stay out of prison. He is a high-level thief and smuggler who has been out of our reach for six years, but not any longer. This is our chance to build a case and get him and he knows it. He is also known for killing people who get in his way of his continuing freedom. We can't afford any mistakes on this one. A lot of people are watching you on this one and it is high profile. Any questions?'

'What time do we take over?'

'As soon as you get there, Sergeant. They are currently in Central Park. They have been in a safe house for weeks. He found them and so we need to move them. It is understood he will not kill them in the open but be on your guard. He will take them if he sees a chance and then all we get are bodies back. We can't find another witness who is willing to do this, so we need to keep her safe. Good luck.'

***

In the cars, Kathy travelled with Bennett and Will. Bennett drove, Will was in the front and Kathy in the back. The rest of the team rode in the second car behind.

'So, what was the name of that blonde you were with last week?' Bennett asked, looking over at Will. Bennett always considered himself a lady's man but couldn't get anyone in the same class as Will, so he was always looking for a way in to the circle that Will was a part of.

'Jennifer, why?' Will responded without looking back at him.

'That's it, Jennifer. Just wondered if you still had her number, if you are done with it, of course. Thought I might give her a call and ask her out.'

'Yeah, I still have it. Remind me when we get back, but you know she will say no, right?' Will replied with a smile.

'What? No way. I can make a woman like that happy.'

'Yeah, right. Of course you can, because you date women like her all the time, right? She is very high maintenance and I'm not so sure you can handle that. Now, can we focus, please? We have a job to do.'

For once, Kathy agreed with him. She tolerated the men's talk when it was in the locker room, but she hated when it carried on past the door, never mind the fact it was about the women that Sergeant Falco was with last.

She needed to get off this team. It was bad enough that she had a school girl crush but now she was getting jealous of his conquests, it was too much for her. All she wanted to do was get on with her job and get her promotion so she could move forward and start leaving these feelings behind.

Will turned round and looked at Kathy in the back. She was looking out the window, deep in thought. Her mind was wandering back to Chicago and her road to now; today could be the start of a new chapter for her. She had moved to Chicago with her fiancée, who worked in the fire department, but she was only twenty-two and had no work or career prospects.

Tony said she didn't have to work, that he would take care of her. She couldn't do nothing though, and she wanted to have purpose, a job that gave her more than just an income, but she wasn't prepared for the reaction she got when she joined the police force.

Her family were completely against it, especially her mother; she was very vocal in her dislike for such a profession and Tony really hated the idea and many arguments followed her decision. She, however, was happy for the first time in her life. She got satisfaction from her job she never had before. She was twenty-seven when her Sergeant approached her about joining SWAT. He had seen her abilities on the job as well as the range. She was thrilled with the idea of being put forward for such a highly respected unit. Tony was not so welcoming to the idea. He became argumentative and dismissive. He tried everything to dissuade her from joining. Her family, of course, were on his side and as she looked back, joining SWAT was the beginning of the end of their relationship.

The next two years were torture. The put downs, the verbal abuse, eventually got too much. When her grandmother died and left

Kathy her house in the will, to the surprise and horror of the rest of the family, she saw an opportunity and put in her transfer for New York.

When she got to New York and found she was put on the sniper team, she was amazed. She had impressed in so many ways in Chicago. When she transferred, the report that New York were given spoke praises to such an extent she was put with the best. Three years later, was all that hard work going to pay off? All the pushing by Sergeant Falco, would it finally be worth it? She really did hope so, she had worked so hard in training, on the range and out on calls, she had got better in all areas and just wanted more than anything for it to be enough.

She was so deep in her thoughts, she didn't notice him looking at her.

'What must she think of me?' he thought. 'All she hears are these constant stories of other women and most of it is just exaggerated men's talk.' He had never denied that he liked the company of women and that he often went out to dinners and parties when it was his weekend off, but sometimes that's all it was.

He must focus on the job. It was too important to mess up, but he couldn't help but think of her.

'Why would she ever want a player like me? She could do so much better. A solid, nice guy would be far better for her, anyone but me,' he thought, as he turned away and got his mind back on the job in hand.

***

When they arrived in Central Park, they were signalled where to go by a detective waiting for them at the entrance. They stopped near to where some children were playing soccer. As they stopped, a few people in the park looked to see what was happening, but they carried on with their days as though nothing was happening, though one or two lingered longer than normal. Will got out and spoke to two detectives, both in everyday clothes, then Will signalled for the team to get out and gave them instructions on where to go.

'Hill, Bennett and Harvey, you will go and collect the family. We will stay here and watch the road and vehicles. Eyes open at all times, he will be watching us,' Will told the team.

Kathy headed off with Bennett and Harvey to where the family were waiting, about thirty metres away from the cars, with two other detectives, again in normal clothes, they didn't stand out at all. Which was the reason it was playing on Kathy's mind: why send uniformed SWAT officers to move a witness to a secret location when the people with her were in plain clothes and no one would notice them at all? Something just felt wrong about this whole thing, and she didn't like it.

As they approached the family, the two young children hid behind their mother, they were only young, aged four and five. The mother was also young, only twenty-four; she was small and thin with dark hair, she looked like the weight of the world was on her and like she hadn't slept for weeks.

'They must be terrified,' claimed Harvey, gesturing to the kids looking at them from behind their mother's legs. 'I know I would be if I were a kid and three strangers were walking towards me with guns, even if we are cops.'

It was at that moment when Kathy did something that her training said not to, but as a woman her instincts insisted on. She took her rifle and put it out of their sight and took her helmet off. She knelt down in front of them and spoke softly, so that only they could hear. Smiles appeared on their faces and they ran off towards the cars. She stood and signalled to the team at the cars. They were moving, then she put her helmet on but failed to fasten it. The mother smiled at Kathy in thanks then followed, walking between Harvey and Bennett with the two detectives in front and Kathy behind. They were heading back across the grass when suddenly something knocked her helmet to the ground. She instinctively went to pick it up and BANG, something hit her hard in the face.

She lay on the grass, a bit dazed, but it didn't take her long to realise there was a gun pointing right at her head.

'Get them in the car,' she heard Will shout, as he, Tom and Palmer came running over, guns pointing at the man who was pointing his gun at her.

'Well, Sergeant Falco, we meet again, though it seems your illustrious team are slipping. I thought getting this close would have been a lot harder than it was, but some of your team just weren't paying attention, were they?' he said, smiling, referring to Kathy lying helpless on the ground.

'What do you want?' Will asked him.

'Why do you ask me questions when you already know the answers?'

'I won't let you take them, you know that,' Will insisted.

'Yes, this time perhaps, but let this be a warning. I can get to them as and when I choose. I will not be locked away by you or anyone, and you of all people should know what happens to people when they get in my way. Bye for now, Sergeant. I will be seeing you real soon.'

He smiled and walked away, his gun on Kathy till he disappeared between the crowds that had gathered around them.

Chapter Four

People started moving on, watching as they went. Many shocked by what they had just witnessed. Will was pacing and looking around.

'You OK?' Tom asked as he pulled her to her feet.

'Yeah, I am fine,' she replied, wiping the blood from her face. She bent down to get her rifle and helmet before letting Tom look at the cut on her face.

'What the hell happened?' Will shouted at her. 'And this had better be good. This could have ruined the whole operation and the case.'

'It was my fault, Sergeant, I let my guard down and he was watching. Ouch! Tom not so hard.'

'Sorry, just trying to stop the bleeding,' Tom said while pressing a handkerchief on the cut.

'Well, you can sort that out at the safe house. Let's go before something else goes wrong,' Will said, his voice full of anger. He walked off ahead to the cars, looking around, but the man he was searching for was gone.

'He sounds really pissed,' exclaimed Palmer. 'Even more than normal.'

'Really?' commented Tom. 'You don't say. This was meant to be an easy day and a quick and smooth hand over.'

'Sorry guys, this was my fault, I should not have taken my helmet off and I wasn't paying attention.'

'Kathy, it's all right, we all make mistakes,' Tom responded. 'It's just that with this guy, it is very personal, and every time we seem to get close to getting him, or we answer a call where he is involved, he always seems to escape or something goes wrong. Sergeant Falco won't rest till we finally get him and he is either dead or locked away for good.'

They started walking towards the cars.

'So, let's get in the cars, get to the safe house, fix your face and finish up. I can't wait for this one to be over.'

'I won't argue with that,' Kathy replied.

***

The safe house was a third-floor apartment in a renovated warehouse just over the river. It was a secure building, with CCTV and electronic locks on the doors. It was also a new location. It had to be, there had been so much witness tampering on this case already and they had also lost witnesses to date, they couldn't afford to lose any more. This witness had to testify before a grand jury and then they had to catch him, which was proving impossible. He never seemed to appear anywhere that he could get caught, like today; he wouldn't have hesitated to shoot Kathy had Will gone to shoot him or arrest him.

The operation was not over for the team until they were safely inside and witness protection team had arrived to take over.

'This is only temporary until we can move you out of state, but you will be safe here. There will be someone here with you around the clock, and it will only take a few days before you can make a permanent move,' Will explained to the witness as Kathy and Tom entered.

They were the last up and all was secure.

'Thank you so much,' she replied, relieved and thankful that they would finally be safe, and she could relax for the first time in weeks.

'You are welcome, but we are just doing our job,' Will replied. It was times like this that made all the harder parts of the job completely worth it. He just hoped that they and the witness protection team could keep her safe

Kathy headed straight to the bathroom to look at her face.

'Damn.' She shook her head as she looked in the mirror. It wasn't a big cut but it was a big mistake and she knew it.

'I can't believe I was that stupid. When this gets back to the Captain, I will never make team leader,' she said to her own reflection.

She wiped the blood off her face, took a deep breath and headed back out to the living area. The team were stood talking at the breakfast bar that separated the kitchen and the lounge, Harvey was making some warm drinks. The witness was settling her children into one of the two bedrooms and Will was stood by the window in the lounge deep in thought and watching the street below.

Will was clearly angered and frustrated by what had happened earlier in the park. He heard her come out of the bathroom, he looked over and snapped at her.

'Get Tom to look at that cut and then go and stand outside the door to keep watch. I don't want anything else to go wrong today. Witness protection will be here very soon so let's do the job right till then.'

'My head is fine, I just had a look in the bathroom and...'

'I said get Tom to look at it. It is still bleeding,' he retorted before she could finish.

She was getting frustrated too and as she raised her voice, the team looked in shock at the developing situation.

'And I said it was fine, so I will be outside the door if you need me.'

No one in his team had ever spoken to him like that before, or not followed an order he had given. They were his rules, and he was not in the mood for that to change today, he had got rid of team members for less. She headed out of the door and he followed her, slamming it behind him. The room fell silent till Bennett spoke.

'Wow, never seen him so mad and that is saying something.'

'Me neither,' agreed Palmer. 'What do you suppose will happen?' he questioned, looking straight at Tom.

'How the hell do I know?' he answered.

'Well, you know him better than any of us,' Harvey commented, handing out the coffees he had made.

'Maybe so but that doesn't mean I know what he is going to say or do. I'm no mind reader and my advice would be stay the hell out of it, drink your coffees and don't set foot outside that door till he comes back in.'

Chapter Five

Outside the front door of the apartment was quite dark and there were no lights on to avoid it being noticed from the outside as being occupied. No one else lived on that floor which had been deliberate on the part of the police so neighbours didn't start asking questions, but there was noise coming from the stairs and floors below. The stairs were about ten metres away from the door. Kathy walked to the top and looked down to make sure there was no one around or coming up them; she saw some teenagers heading down chatting as they went. Suddenly, the door slammed. Kathy jumped and turned round to see Will looking at her furiously.

'What the hell are you doing?' he blasted at her.

Kathy said nothing, just looked back at him. She didn't want to do this here or now, she knew she would get pulled later for the way she had just spoke to him but she hoped he would let that happen back at the office.

'Well, do I get an answer?' he said sternly.

She took a deep breath. 'I came out to watch the door, just like you told me. Just following orders, Sergeant,' she replied calmly, but with a hint of sarcasm.

'I also told you to get your head checked but I don't see you doing that,' he replied with the same level of sarcasm.

'That is because it is fine and let's be fair here, I should know if it is.' Frustration was beginning to build up inside her.

'I still want it looked at and patched up. It is still bleeding,' Will insisted.

'It's my head, and what the hell do you care anyway?' she snapped.

'It may be your head, but you are on my team and this op is too important to screw up, so go inside and get Tom to look at it like I said before. At least have a band-aid put on it. I will stay here till you get back.'

She was getting really annoyed now. Why the hell did he have to follow her out here? She just wanted some peace, and how dare he? Work was all he cared about and she had had enough of him not being bothered about her, in any way. He hadn't even asked if she was OK. It was like she wasn't even part of the team anymore. She felt it was about time she stood up for herself and tell him just how she felt. It may lose her the chance to lead a team but after today, that boat had probably already sailed. She needed to say what was on her mind or she never would, then continuing to work with him every day would be a nightmare.

'Yes, of course,' she started. She could feel all her anger coming to the surface. 'The operation, because God forbid, I should screw that up for YOU. It's only my head, no one important. I mean, it's YOUR team, YOUR op, and, let's face it, that is all that matters to YOU. You have pushed me out of this team bit by bit over the last year, and well, it looks like you are free of me because after this major fuck up, I am sure you have all you need to get rid of me, don't you?' She turned away and moved towards the window.

Will just stood there looking at her for a moment, not really knowing what to say. He had no idea that is how he had made her feel, it was never his intention; he had been trying to protect them both, from being hurt.

'Where the hell did all that come from? If you aren't happy on the team, you should have come to me, had a conversation, not wait and let it all build up,' he finally said, calmly.

She turned to face him. 'That is how you have made me feel, especially this last year and I don't care if you try and deny it. You have pushed me out of the team. I used to feel like one of the guys but now things have changed, and I feel like an outsider, so how could I possibly come and talk to you? I even considered changing teams a few months ago but the Captain told me not to and try and stick it out, because you are a good team leader, he said, but you demand the best,' she replied, taking another deep breath to calm her frustration.

Should she have let it come out quite like that, she wondered. Maybe not, but it was too late now, so she waited for him to respond.

He looked at her in amazement. She looked so beautiful at that moment, so strong but vulnerable at the same time. He thought about the last few months and it was true, he had pushed her out but not because he didn't care but because he could feel himself caring too much, and with the job they did, the close proximity they worked in, the life and death situations they faced each day, he had pushed those feelings way down inside, hoping no one would see what he really felt. He didn't want this though, not this anger; he hadn't realised how it had affected her and he was ashamed to admit it too. He just had to figure out now what he could say that could make this all OK.

'I would never try and get you off my team, but you can leave if that's what you really want, but it's not what I want you to do,' he finally said.

Kathy stepped forward and went to speak.

'Let me finish, here, sit down.' He took a chair that was by the door and sat her on it. 'You are one of the best people I have ever had on my team and as for today, we all make mistakes.'

'What, even you?' she asked, looking up at him.

'Especially me. Ask the Captain. How many times have you seen me pulled into the office over the last few years? I have just got better at cleaning up my mess, and making less mistakes but we have to make mistakes or how could we ever learn from them? And as for being perfect, I am far from it. I push my team hard so that they try and be the best, to show them what they are capable of achieving if they work hard and improve their skills.'

He crouched down in front of her, took a handkerchief out of his pocket and started gently wiping the blood from her face.

'Don't worry, its clean. I always have one with me. There is nothing worse than having a cold and not having one with you in this job.'

He looked her straight in the eyes and smiled, a smile she had never seen before, so soft and caring, a side of him very few people ever got to see.

'And as far as not caring about you, of course I do. How could I not?' He paused, not knowing if he should continue. 'But I had no choice but to distance myself from you. We work together, we have to rely on each other in pressure situations, and it is the only way I could stop myself from...' he paused and looked at her, searching to see if he should continue.

'From what?'

'From this.'

At that moment, he kissed her, as soft and gentle as the smile he had before it.

He stood up quickly and took a step back.

'Shit, I should not have done that. Sorry, I just can't do this.' He shook his head. 'You are a clever, beautiful woman, but this can't happen.'

'I don't understand.' She looked at him, confused, searching for an explanation.

'I wouldn't want my feelings to affect your future in the team or the unit. It's selfish and I couldn't do that, not to you.'

'And if I want this too?'

'I can't be selfish again. I'm sorry.'

Kathy suddenly jumped up from the chair and reached for the gun at her side.

'Don't even think about it,' said the voice she recognised from the park. He stepped out of the darkness of the stairway. 'Very touching, Sergeant. Now turn around with your hands on your head.'

Will turned round to see him pointing a gun at them both.

'Now I had come for my friend in there, but a new idea just hit me. Now come here,' he ordered in Kathy's direction.

She hesitated then she slowly walked over, looking at Will as she went.

'Now turn around slowly.'

There were two other men with him, armed and pointing their guns right at Kathy. So all Will could do was watch as he disarmed her. He looked her up and down.

'I can see we are going to have some fun.'

'It would be just one more reason for me to kill you,' Will snapped back.

'Promises, promises, Sergeant. Now I recall you said that to me repeatedly over the last six years, and I am still here. You just don't seem to be capable of catching me now, do you?' he smirked. 'Now I will call you in two hours on this.' He threw a cell phone at Will. 'I will give you instructions, which if you follow, you MAY just see your girlfriend here again.'

He forced Kathy to the top of the stairs, his two men behind aiming at Will. Then they were gone.

Will ran into the apartment shouting 'He's got Hill, let's go.'

Chapter Six

Will went down the stairs followed by Tom and Bennett, checking for any sign of them as they went, checking every corridor on each floor. Palmer and Harvey stayed with the witness, in case it was a decoy to get to her. When they got down to the front door, they met the officers who had come to take over.

'Did anyone leave the building as you were arriving?' Will questioned.

'No,' he paused. 'Wait, there was a cleaning crew but that's all.'

'Which way did they go? WHICH WAY?' Will shouted at them.

'They went round to the alley just left to the building.' The team ran out the door. 'What the hell is going on?' the officer called after them but they had gone.

The alley ran down the left side of the building and connected to main roads at both ends. It was full of garbage ready for collection, but was still quite wide; when they arrived, there was no sign of anyone at all.

'Damn it!' shouted Will in frustration, punching a nearby garbage can. He started walking up and down thinking, but furious with himself and with him. Will couldn't believe this was happening. He couldn't help but feel responsible yet again and those voices of self-doubt started to whisper again.

'What the hell happened up there?' Tom asked. 'How the hell did he know where we were? Why didn't you see them coming up the stairs? You never take your eyes off the job for a second. What happened?'

'ME, that's what happened,' Will screamed back at Tom. He was obviously not in the mood for questions. He walked off back towards the main street, to go back upstairs, leaving Tom and Bennett looking at each other in complete confusion.

***

The SWAT office was on the first floor of the police department building, on the far end. It had the indoor range, gun cage and gym underneath them as well as a garage for the vehicles. The office was simple in décor, it had eight groups of five desks, one for each team, and then one spare set. The team leaders all had an office around the edge. Will's team had their desks closest to the door, they got more calls than any other team and so had to be in the most accessible place, but Will's office was on the back wall, next to the Captain. Many said it was so the Captain could keep a closer eye on him, but if you asked him, it was because he was Alpha Team leader so needed to be there. There was a coffee machine close to the door and a television above it, which was used for a variety of reasons but its purpose was for work.

All the team, except for Will, headed straight up to the office when they got back. They were all shocked by what had just happened, but they had reports to write, though not quite sure what to say in them. They were also tired and ready to go home. Will headed for the gym to relieve some frustration and to avoid the Captain as long as he could.

'Where is he?' questioned the Captain as he approached Tom and the others from across the office.

'Punching the life out of the bag in the gym, Sir,' Harvey responded.

'He hasn't spoken all the way back, but I am sure he will be up soon, he just needs to vent some anger and frustration first,' Tom continued.

'Well I want him up here now and I want someone to tell me what happened and how.'

'We don't know, sir. We were in the apartment with the witness,' explained Palmer. 'Sergeant Falco was outside the door with Hill. We didn't know anything till he came in saying he had taken her. We never even heard anything.'

'Was it him, Hargreaves?' the Captain asked quietly.

'Yes, Sir, at the park and the apartment. He must have been tipped off somehow, though we don't know by who or why. He really has it in for the Sergeant, especially after the jewellery store incident, but why he took Hill I don't know, it doesn't make any sense, unless he just saw an opportunity with her being on our team. We don't know why they weren't seen coming either, what they were doing, only Sergeant Falco can answer that one.'

'Then get him up here to my office so I can ask him myself,' Captain Bridge ordered.

***

Down in the gym Will had stopped for a moment and sat drinking some water when Tom walked in. The gym wasn't big but had enough space and equipment for what it was used for. Will had been there quite often over the last few years, since his parents were killed. He had many issues with anger and emotions he had never had before. It was grief, he supposed, but maybe there was also some guilt thrown in. It was his oasis when things had gone bad or when he was frustrated by the red tape and politics.

Will signalled to the other officers in there to leave, he didn't want anyone hearing something that could be used against him, or worse, risk the life of Kathy, but he knew he had to give Tom some kind of explanation and he wanted to tell him everything, but he didn't know where to start and he wanted to get it all straight in his head before telling him or the Captain.

'Captain wants to see you,' Tom said as he approached.

'So, what's new?' Will responded. 'I will be up when I'm ready.'

'I don't get it, man, what happened?'

'I don't want to talk about it right now, so why don't you go and write up and I will be up when I'm done?' Will responded.

'Will, you have to talk about it eventually. I have never seen you like this, even when an op has gone wrong before, not since... you know. Why did he take Kathy? He had no reason to, did he? I mean, this time it's different from before, right?' Tom looked questioningly at Will.

'He took her because I screwed up.' He stood up and continued, 'I should have kept my feelings in check but...' he shook his head. 'He saw me kiss her. You happy, now you know why?' He turned round and put his water down.

'You did what?' Tom was taken aback. He had only known Will to put his feelings before the job once before, and he was beginning to see why Will was so stressed out; he knew this was serious and not just some crush. 'What was in your head? Why did you not talk to me? You always tell me stuff like this. So, what do we do now?'

Will turned round, he stood defensively and looked at him.

'I didn't tell you because it would have affected the team, and I wasn't really sure what

69

you would think. I know you don't like most of the women I date and they are never serious and I didn't want you to think I would treat Kathy in a similar way. I should never have done what I did today and now he has her, which right now, I can't change, and I hate myself for putting her in that position, but all we can do now is write up our reports, tell the Captain what happened and wait for this to ring,' he said, as he took the cell phone out of his pocket. It was going to ring in just one hour.

***

Will spent the next fifty minutes in the captain's office going over the events of the day again and again. Voices raised and then they went very quiet again, but the team could only speculate as to what was being said inside.

'Tom, my office,' Will said as he came out.

The Captain stood at his door and shouted to Will, 'Sergeant, is this going to be a regular thing?'

Will turned and smiled before he replied, 'It won't happen again, Sir, you have my word on that.'

The team looked at each other, trying to work out exactly what was going on, but they had learned with Sergeant Falco not to ask those kinds of questions.

Tom followed Will into his office and closed the door behind him. Will's office was small with only enough room for his desk, two chairs, one either side and a filing cabinet. Will sat in his chair and started looking through some papers on his desk.

'What's up? What's going on, Will?'

Will looked up at Tom. 'He's going to call any minute.'

'What? Did you tell the Captain?' Tom asked, sitting opposite Will and leaning forward onto the desk.

'No, I didn't tell him, and I didn't tell him about the cell phone. Now keep your voice down.' He took it out of his pocket and put it on the desk. 'I have to answer the phone or she is dead. I can't risk that, not yet, and besides it was hard enough telling him how all this happened in the first place, but I will tell him when we know more, that's if there is any way I can. Something tells me that it won't be in his best interests so will probably stop us from doing so.'

'He is going to find out. Then what?'

Tom sat back in his chair, he was getting worried just how deep they were getting in this and what lengths they were going to have to go to get out.

'Not sure yet, that's why, till we need to include anyone else, it is just you and me on this. We have to try and control this the best we can. It's the best thing, especially for Kathy. You have my back, right?'

'I can't believe you have to ask that.' He shook his head and paused, looking at the cell. 'This is way above our heads. Are you sure this is how you want to do it?'

At that moment, the phone rang. They both looked at it, then at each other. Will took a deep breath and answered it.

'Hello?' He picked up a pen, so as to get every detail.

'Hello, Sergeant, are you ready for what I need you to do tomorrow?'

'Yes, I am.'

'You will go to work and carry on as normal.'

'What?' He wasn't sure what was going on but he expected more than that.

'Well, Sergeant, due to my change in plan, I need an extra day to get sorted and so I want you to go to work as normal tomorrow. Now I will be listening in to the scanner so will know if for any reason, you are trying to find me or something. That wouldn't be good for your girlfriend's health here. I will call back tomorrow at the same time.'

He hung up before he had got chance to reply or to ask to speak to Kathy.

'So, what does he want?' Tom asked impatiently.

'For us to go to work as normal and he will call same time tomorrow. He will be listening in to the scanners to ensure we don't try finding them,' Will answered despondently.

'I don't get it.'

'He wants me to sweat. He won't give her up easily until he is sure he has got away with it. He wants me to be on edge and screw up, but I will not let him win, not this time.'

'OK, so we are done. Do you want a beer? You can unwind and maybe it will help you get some sleep. I know you and you will only obsess if you go home.'

'Yeah, sure, think I need one.'

Chapter Seven

Will and Tom decided to go for a quiet drink in their favourite bar, it was Tuesday so not many officers would be there tonight, which meant the need for small talk would be reduced greatly. They walked across the road together after getting changed. Charlie's bar was open every night, Will and Tom had been going there since they joined the force; it wasn't the biggest, but it had a pool table at the bottom end, a small bar up by the door and about twenty small tables with chairs and another twenty-five bar stools at the bar itself and various high tables including in the window.

When they entered, there was Charlie behind the bar as always and there were two men playing pool who they didn't recognise. Will went to the bar and Tom sat at a table.

'Charlie, can I get two beers please?'

'Sure thing, Falco,' replied Charlie.

'Quiet tonight,' Will said, looking around the bar.

'Yeah, except a couple of tourists,' he said, gesturing towards the pool table. 'Don't get many regulars from the PD on a Tuesday.'

He put the beers on the bar and Will paid him. 'Thanks, Charlie,' he said, taking them and heading to the table where Tom was sat.

He sat in the chair opposite. They didn't speak for a few moments but Tom couldn't stand the silence.

'So, what did the Captain say? You never said.'

'Not much, just wanted to know what happened.'

'That's all?'

'Yeah, he was not happy of course, especially as he has got the jump on us twice and so we will see what happens with that.'

'Does he think someone tipped off our locations?'

'I don't know, but it feels like he is playing us and I don't know how to get Kathy back without playing along.'

'So we just do what he says in hope she is still alive?'

'Well that depends on what he wants us to do, doesn't it? I think he will keep her while he pulls a job, but I might be wrong.' Will took a long drink.

'We will see what happens tomorrow,' Tom said.

'Yeah, and are we set for the weekend? I mean if this is over?'

'Of course, it's your birthday and I will be there with you as always, and it will be over, I am sure.'

Will and Tom had got together for Will's birthday for the last five years, they visited his parents' graves then had a meal in their favourite restaurant. Lynne, Tom's wife, would often join them for the meal but Will usually went alone. His parents had been killed buying his birthday gift and it was a difficult time of year for them both.

Will got up and headed to the rest rooms at the back of the bar; he past the two men playing pool. On his way back past, he knocked the cue by accident.

'Sorry,' he said, then he headed back to the table.

'Hey,' one of them shouted after him. 'Hey, I'm talking to you.'

Will turned around to see a man just a bit older than him, but he was just five-foot-six, his red hair was thinning on top and he was a little round around his waist. His friend stood just behind him, taller at five-foot-ten, completely grey, in his forties, but trimmer than the other one.

'What?' Will responded.

'You just knocked my cue as you went past.'

'Yes, and I apologised, so I am not sure what your problem is.'

'You ruined my whole shot,' he shouted.

'Come on, you can retake it,' his friend said, trying to pull him away.

'I suggest you go back with your friend and carry on with your game,' Will said very calmly.

'Why? You think I should be scared of you or something? What, because you are bigger than me, you think you can push me around?'

Tom stood up and came over.

'Listen, guys, we just want a quiet drink after a rough shift, so if you don't mind, we would like to get back to it,' Tom said.

'Rough shift? Why, what do you do?' said the taller one.

'We are police officers,' Tom replied.

'So that's why you think you can push us around, is it?' he started again.

Just then, Charlie came over. 'Listen, guys, I don't want any trouble. You either carry on with your game or you leave.'

'Us, leave?' he said, outraged. 'What did we do?'

'Come on, let's just get back to the game,' the taller one said as he pulled his friend away towards the pool table.

Charlie followed them over to make sure that was the end of it.

'Listen, guys, Sergeant Falco there is a regular and he is not a man to piss off, OK?'

'Why's that?'

'He's SWAT, and one of the best there is. Word from the other guys I get in here from the PD, him and his team are the top team over there and shoot more bad guys than all the others put together, and he is also a very good friend. I have known him for years.'

The two men looked over at Will and Tom as they finished their drinks and headed out of the bar.

Outside the bar, Tom stopped.

'You OK?' he asked, gesturing back at the bar.

'Yeah, I'm heading home. Don't worry, I am not going to shoot anyone tonight.' He smiled and walked over to the PD car park and collected his motorbike.

Chapter Eight

Will had hardly slept and was on his third cup of coffee when the rest of the team walked in the office. Will had been sat in his office for the last hour going over reports from the previous day and past cases to see if he could figure out where he would be holding Kathy. Truth was, he had come up with nothing, and he had to face a whole day at work without being able to get anywhere. He came out of his office and walked over to get another coffee.

'Morning, guys, hope you all slept well. Could be a long one today, especially with us being one short. I need your A game.'

Just then Captain Bridge appeared, followed by an officer from internal affairs who Will recognised well.

'Why do you think he's here?' Bennett asked.

'Has to be about yesterday,' Tom replied.

They went into the Captain's office and closed the door behind them.

'So, any news yet, Sergeant, from whoever is looking for Kathy?' asked Palmer.

'No, nothing yet,' answered Will. 'But I am sure there will be something soon, he can't hide her forever.'

They were all sat round the desks talking, when the Captain's door opened. The Captain came out.

'Sergeant Falco, can you come in my office for a minute?'

Will got up, looked at Tom and went over to the Captain. He went in and the Captain followed, closing the door.

'Internal affairs have graced us with their presence. Apparently, they are looking into the incident yesterday and they are looking at you and your team,' said Captain Bridge as he walked back round behind his desk.

'Seriously?' Will said, folding his arms across his chest.

'Well, Sergeant, why don't you sit down and we can discuss the matter further?' said Lieutenant Green.

'I'm OK standing, thanks.'

'OK. We know there is a leak somewhere. Your team knew both locations and timings, so

I am here to find out if it's you or a member of your team.'

'You actually believe one of us is responsible for the kidnapping of our own team member?'

'It's possible.'

'It's bullshit!' Will shouted.

'Sergeant, watch yourself,' Captain Bridge intervened. 'Lieutenant, you know this makes no sense.'

'They could have done it for the money. Even a Sergeant's pay isn't that good.'

Will laughed. 'Money? That's your motive? Well, good luck with that.'

'What I do know, Sergeant, is over the next few days, I will be scrutinising your team and this unit until I have cleared you, and one bad shoot and I will have your badge.'

Just then, Will's radio went.

'We have armed assailants in a clothing store down on fifth avenue.'

'Alpha Team on route,' Will responded. 'Excuse me, Lieutenant, I have real work to go and do,' he said, then walked out. They watched him cross the office.

'Come on, guys, let's go.' And with that they left.

Lieutenant Green and Captain Bridge stood at his office door.

'He will bring this whole unit down, Captain. He is hot headed and arrogant, and worse than that, he doesn't care who he takes down with him.'

'Lieutenant, you don't know Sergeant Falco. He is a fantastic officer and he is the best this office has. So, if you are looking to take down him and his team, you had better watch yourself because that will not go down well in this office or across the NYPD. This city is safer because of officers like him.'

'Captain, I hope that's not a threat.'

'No, Lieutenant, it's a promise. Now, I too have work to do, so show yourself out.'

***

They arrived in their cars, another team had taken the truck for training outside the city. They stopped a block down and got out.

'What we got?' Will asked.

'Sergeant Falco, how are you? Heard about Kathy, sorry man,' replied Sergeant Edwards. They had known each other for a few years, meeting on incidents and having the odd beer together after shift.

'Cheers. We will get her back.'

'Of course, you will. Now, we have two armed assailants in a luxury leather goods store.'

'OK, so what's the front like? Any vantage points?'

'It's glass fronted, but they have a display in the window.' He paused. 'We aren't really sure what's going on in there. They don't have much money on the premises at this time of day, and there have been no demands.'

'Have you cleared their line of sight from inside?'

'Yeah we have, even the cops.'

'Good, here's what I think: me and Tom approach from this side and go in the front door. My other three cover the sides.'

'Sounds good to me, Sergeant.'

Tom and Will approached the store, the door and front were all glass so they had to be careful. Will knew the store and the owner, he could see two people in front of the counter, behind which the owner was stood. It appeared the two were holding weapons, but they looked different, he could also see at least two customers in the back of the store.

'OK,' he whispered to Tom, 'there are two with weapons, the owner and I think two customers at the back. It looks like someone has been throwing paint around or something. I will see if I can get the owner to make them look towards the back so we can enter from here.'

Will took his phone out and text her, he knew she kept her phone on the counter and that she kept it on silent when working. He saw her glance down at the phone. She started to move down the counter and they started to turn; when the door was out of their line of sight, Will signalled to Tom and they entered through the front door. Will went in first and Tom stopped just inside the door while Will moved forward.

'NYPD, put your weapons down and turn around slowly,' Will shouted.

The two assailants turned around, there was a male, he was five-foot-ten with thick dark blond hair and thick stubble, he was quite heavy and had a nervous look about him. The female was not much over five foot two, she had long, thin bright pink hair and black make up, her skin was so pale, it was almost white and she was so thin she looked like she could break at any time.

'They are just paintball guns,' she whimpered.

Will assessed them, they were an odd couple indeed.

'Why are you in a clothing store firing paintballs at things?' Will asked

'We are against using animals for clothing or to eat, and this is our protest against the cruelty' she stated but rather quietly.

'No,' Will replied 'a protest is quietly walking around outside with placards chanting or something. What we have here is criminal damage and therefore, you two are under arrest'

'Under arrest?' the man said with a hint of a non-American accent, his voice harsh and showing his anger.

'Yeah,' said Will, 'so put your paintball guns on the counter and put your hands on your heads.'

They both put their paintball guns on the counter, the female put her hands on her head, but the man pulled a handgun from the back of his jeans and pointed it at Will. The female looked at him in shock, it was clear she knew nothing about this actual gun he now held.

'No, we are going to walk out of here and carry on with our protest of stores that sell animal products,' he said.

Will looked across at Tom and smiled, his weapon pointing at the assailants the whole time.

'Really?' Will said as he turned back to look at them. 'You wouldn't get a foot out of that door. You see, you have just that one gun and even if you managed to get one shot off, you would most likely miss and I would shoot you.'

'Why do you presume I would miss?'

'Even if you hit me, my man over here would put you down or one of the other three of my team outside would, so you can put the gun down or I can put you in the hospital, or the morgue.'

'You are just trying to scare me.'

'Do you really think, as SWAT officers, we would miss you? Really?'

'You can't shoot me for nothing, I know the law.'

'Well, look it up again, you are pointing a gun at a police officer, threatening to fire. I am allowed to fire first if you refuse to put it down, so put the gun down.'

'No,' he said. 'We are leaving'

'OK, last chance. Drop the gun or I will fire.'

'NO!' he shouted.

Will glanced at Tom, nodded then fired. The round went straight through his right shoulder, he fell to the ground. The woman screamed and bent down to him, her hand reached for the gun he had dropped.

'I suggest you don't do that,' Will said.

She looked up to see him stood right in front of her, gun pointing right at her. She stood and stepped back.

'We are all clear control, we need an EMT and we need officers to escort the two assailants, as they are both under arrest,' Will radioed through.

Then, as the officers and EMT entered the shop, Tom opened the door for them, the customers came from the back of the store and over to Will. Will recognised one of them, the man from Charlie's the night before that had tried to start a fight with him; he had a woman with him, Will guessed it was his wife. She was about the same height, with highlighted bobbed hair, she was really quite beautiful, though she had eyes that said she had been through a lot in her life.

'We just wanted to say thanks' she said. 'We can't quite believe what just happened, we only came in for some boots.'

'Just doing my job,' replied Will.

'Thanks, anyway,' the man said holding out his hand. Will shook it and they left with an officer to give their statement.

'Will Falco, look at you, you're looking good, not seen you in uniform before, it suits you.'

'Rachel,' he said as he turned to face her. 'Long time no see, thanks for the assist.'

'You are welcome,' she smiled. 'Glad it was you that came out though, I know you said you were a cop, but it was hard to believe without seeing it.'

'Well what can I say, they sent the best, and you haven't seen me in uniform before because you haven't needed to.'

'And I am grateful for that. Seriously though, how long till I can sort out and clean this place up because it's going to take me ages to get that bloody paint out and this blood, well, that's even worse.'

'Well, it shouldn't take too long, sorry about the blood.'

'Not your fault, some of these people go too far.'

'Well, tell you what, get some professional cleaners in and send me the bill, OK?' he smiled 'Now don't forget to give your statement and I will see you at the black and white dinner next month.'

'Yes, for sure, will save you a dance. Goodbye, Sergeant Falco.'

Will left and Tom followed him.

'I am not going to ask how well you know her.'

'Good, because I don't want to discuss it.'

'That sure was fun though, some of these protesters really take the piss, I wonder if they really know what they are doing sometimes.'

'Well a couple of people can be the exception. I mean, you think of all the protests that go without any trouble, including animal rights, but then you get a few nut jobs who think they can do what they want.'

'True, well, let's get back because I could murder a coffee.'

'Yeah, me too,' Will laughed.

They got back in their cars and headed off.

Chapter Nine

On their way back, Will's phone rang, it was Captain Bridge.

'Sergeant, I know you usually say no, but I have a request from SVU on an arrest warrant, they asked for you.'

'What's the location?' Will replied. 'Tell them we are on our way.'

'I will forward you the location now, Sergeant.'

Will hung up and waited for his phone to beep.

'Tom, pull over till we get a location.'

'What are we doing?'

'Arrest warrant.'

'Really? You hate those.'

'Yeah well, keeping busy will help me get through this day, so if this is what does that, then so be it.'

The phone beeped. Will showed Tom the location and then sent it through to Harvey in the other car.

'Let's go, then,' Tom said as he set off again.

***

They pulled up outside an apartment block in the Bronx. There was a handful of detectives waiting for them to arrive.

'Sergeant Falco, you don't usually grace us with your presence, even when I request you.'

'Yeah, well, slow day, so why not help you lesser mortals with our skills?' Will laughed.

Sergeant Simmons had known Will for ten years, they had always got on and had a lot of respect for each other.

'So, we have a suspect in apartment 3D, he is wanted on multiple rape charges.'

Will looked up at the building.

'Do they have fire escapes for each apartment?' Will asked

'Yeah, think so.'

'Do we know which one is for that apartment or where they come out?'

'They are all down the side of the building, but I don't know which is which.'

'OK, Harvey, Palmer and Bennett, go up with the detectives. Tom, you come with me and we will cover the fire escapes, he is bound to make a run for it down one of them.'

'OK, Sergeant, sounds good.'

'Harvey, take point on entry.'

'No problem, Sergeant.'

As they went up, Will and Tom went round the side of the building, being careful not to be seen.

'So, which fire escape do you think it is?'

'Well, he said 3D so guessing forth one in.'

'So how do we do this?'

'You go above, and I stay a floor below.'

They went up the fire escape as quiet as they could, which was not easy as it was metal and they got themselves into position.

'We are all set,' Will said into his radio.

Next thing, they heard shouting from inside. Then the window opened and a white male climbed out; he came down the fire escape and when he saw Will, turned round but Tom had come down behind him. He stopped and put his hands on his head.

'Now here's a guy who's done this before,' Will said. 'We have the suspect on the fire escape,' he said into his radio.

Sergeant Simmons appeared from the open window.

'Great job guys, could do with you more often.'

'Thanks, Simmons, but we will see.'

***

They got back to the office and as they headed in, Will could see Lieutenant Green in the Captain's office. He grabbed a coffee and headed for his office, went in, left the door open and sat at his desk and started to write up his reports. Captain Bridge appeared at his door.

'What can I do for you, Captain?'

'Heard you did good on that arrest warrant, it does you good when you play well with other departments.'

'Yeah, well, it takes my mind off things, but don't expect it too often,' he paused and sat back in his chair. 'So, what does he want?'

'To talk to you about your first shout this morning.'

'OK,' he got up. 'Let's get it over with.'

They walked from Will's to the Captain's office and shut the door behind them.

'So, Sergeant, I said I would be back but I didn't think it would be so soon. Tell me, is it common practice to shoot people who are carrying paintball guns?'

Will laughed and shook his head. 'He had a hand gun and he pulled it on me when I said they were under arrest, he wouldn't put it down and I gave him three warnings.'

'Says you, Sergeant.'

'Yeah and Hargreaves, plus three witnesses, who will all tell you the same thing,' his voice raising.

'I will check those reports and you had better watch your tone with me, Sergeant, but tell me, did you have to destroy his shoulder to the point he is now in surgery to have it repaired?'

'Better that than in the morgue,' Will replied.

'Well, Captain, I have a feeling I will be back yet again.'

He got up and walked out, looking at Will as he went, who was stood by the door; he was only five-foot-eight and had a very slight frame so he was nothing compared to Will physically.

'I am hoping it was a good shoot, Sergeant,' the Captain said when Lieutenant Green was out of ear shot.

'Yes, Captain, it was. I swear, ask Hargreaves, I didn't want to shoot him but he gave me no choice.'

'OK, get your reports done and I will deal with Green,' he stood up. 'So, out of curiosity what does he have against you?'

'I slept with his wife a few years back.'

'Falco, I might have known, no wonder he has been on this department's ass for the last year or more.'

'I didn't know who she was, but they got divorced soon after, and me and his ex-wife are good friends now actually, but he still blames me.'

'Well, I can understand that, but it gives me an idea, shut the door on your way out.'

***

Will had finished writing his reports for the morning when his phone rang.

'Sergeant, I have someone down at the front desk wanting to speak with you.'

'OK, I will come straight down.'

Will headed down the stairs and through the security door to the front desk.

'They are just over there, Sergeant.' he gestured to two women sat in the waiting area.

'And they are?' Will asked. 'They asked for me?'

'Well they actually asked for the tall, arrogant SWAT officer who shot the boyfriend,' he smiled. 'So, I figured that was you.'

'Thanks a lot, but it could have been Tom, he's tall.'

'Never heard him called arrogant, though.'

'Fair point.'. Will walked over to the two women sat down. As he got closer, Will recognised one of them as the woman from the clothing store that morning; She looked different but he wasn't sure why. She was with another woman who was about five-foot-nine, with dark hair that was cut into a short bob, and she was broad and curvy, and looked very angry.

'Is this him?' she asked the smaller one.

She nodded, barely looking up, she seemed even more withdrawn than before. Almost scared.

'I want an explanation,' she said loudly and in a rather nasty tone.

'About what?' Will responded, arms folded standing tall.

'You shot my niece's boyfriend and had my niece arrested and I want an explanation right now.'

'Well, your niece here committed criminal damage and her boyfriend had a gun.'

'They had paintball guns and were protesting animal rights, what right do you have to shoot anyone in such a way, I will have your badge!' she shouted at him.

Some other officers and civilians had stopped to watch as she got louder. The officers were not sure what Will would do, they knew he wasn't good in confrontation and he didn't take to anyone shouting at him.

'Well now, let's see here, your niece and her boyfriend walked into that clothing store of their own free will, no one forced them. They chose to commit criminal damage, because no matter how you want to dress it up, that is what it is. The owner of that store has the right not to have thousands of dollars' worth of stock damaged.'

She went to speak but he put up his hand to stop her and continued.

'Her boyfriend took a hand gun into that store and pointed it right at me. I asked him three times to put it down and he refused, so yes, I shot him. Which, by law as a SWAT officer, I am allowed to do if I believe people are at risk. The choices they made forced me to make the choice I did.'

'His shoulder is destroyed, you could have killed him.'

'No, I would not have killed him.'

'Of course, you could have, you could have easily got it wrong and missed and killed him.'

'If I had, in fact, wanted to kill him, then he would be dead, I work on SWAT and believe me, I never miss.'

The woman stood there, mouth open in stunned silence at his last remark. Will's radio went.

'Alpha Team leader, we have a hostage situation in an office building on 34th street.'

'Show us as on route, control' Will replied, he turned to the two women 'Excuse me, I have a job to do, if you want to speak to a senior officer, I can send someone down.'

The older woman nodded and they stood there in silence as Will headed back upstairs.

***

'Come on, guys, let's go, we have a shout,' Will said as he walked in the office

'Sergeant Falco, I have you and two other teams attending this one, will meet you there,' Lieutenant Planter said.

'OK, Lieutenant,' he looked over to Captain Bridge. 'Captain, there are a couple of women who want to speak with you at the front desk,'

'What about?'

'They are apparently unhappy with me shooting that guy this morning, and Captain, good luck, you might need it.' Will walked off smiling.

Chapter Ten

All the teams arrived at the location, it was a tall office block.

'So, what we got, Lieutenant?' asked Will as he got out of the car.

'We have a disgruntled ex of an accountant, whose office is with a firm up on the fifteenth floor.'

'Fifteenth floor?' replied Will. 'I hate these ones, no easy way in.'

'No view from buildings around either, it's all that reflective glass all the way up.'

'Great, so what's the plan, Lieutenant?'

'We are waiting for CCTV and building plans, we had him on the phone but he is distraught and not being very co-operative.'

'Who called it in?'

'Well, an employee got out down the stairs and called us. She said he has shot at least three people and had another eight in a meeting room, including his ex-wife. Apparently, he caught her cheating with someone at work.'

'So, he isn't scared of using his gun.'

'No, so get ready because as soon as we have the plans, we are going in.'

Two minutes later, they had the plans in front of them. Will got Tom to look as well and they went over different scenarios before they decided on how they would go in. Will's team made their way up the stairs to the fifteenth floor, it was a long way, but the elevators had been disconnected. This was why Will kept his team so fit; stairways were part of the job on a very regular basis, especially in Manhattan. Will had a second unit coming up behind his, securing the stairwell and the third secured the lobby.

Will slowly opened the stairway door, he stayed low and looked in. He could see one person on the floor, unfortunately dead. He signalled to his team to go in on the left and right, and to stay low till they had swept the office. They went in as directed. They checked the whole office, they found another two dead. Will could hear voices coming from along a corridor; he signalled to his team to follow him and to clear each office as they went. Every room was clear with one left, the meeting room at the bottom. Will knew he had to make a decision and fast, he looked for another way in and got Tom to check the office next door. Tom entered but came out and signalled there was nothing. Will instructed Tom, Bennett and Palmer to hold outside the office and Harvey to go in with him; he didn't want to overwhelm the suspect. He counted down in silence. Then he kicked open the door.

'NYPD, put the gun down'

Right in front of him, there was a man with a gun which was pointing right at the woman he had right in front of him; she looked terrified. There was another eight people over in the corner, all looking scared.

'Come any closer and I will shoot her!' he screamed.

'Put the gun down and we can all walk out of here, there is no need for anyone else to get hurt,' Will said calmly.

'I don't think so,' he said. 'I already killed three, so don't lie to me about walking out. I know that they will shoot me as soon as I leave.'

'If you put that down, I will make sure you walk out.'

'No,' he replied. 'I came here because she left me for some guy who works here, so I came to talk to her and let her know that's not very nice and they all tried to stop me.'

'You need to put that down.'

'No, I think I will kill her instead.'

His finger moved towards the trigger. A shot fired, the female screamed as the man fell to the floor.

'Suspect down, we are all clear,' Will said despondently into the radio.

Harvey put his hand on Will's shoulder. 'Nothing else you could have done, Sergeant.'

'I know,' said Will but it didn't make it easier. No matter what people thought about him, he didn't like having to kill anyone and in cases like this where it was clear they were mixed up and needed help, he hated it even more.

They headed back out into the main office and, with the rest of the team, headed back to the stairway. As they were leaving, officers and crime scene officers arrived to take control and help the hostages.

Will had been busy all day, he had barely had time to think about Kathy; however, now walking down those stairs, that was the only place his mind could go to. He knew the man that had her was more than capable of killing her. The cell phone would ring soon, and then he would know exactly what he was expected to do to get her back.

***

They got back to the office and Captain Bridge was talking to an officer that Will didn't recognise. All his team were tired and it had been a busy day but they still had reports to write before they finished and Will still had a call to take. The team all sat at their desks, Tom got a coffee and so did Will.

'Won't be long now before he calls,' Will said. 'We have thirty minutes, so come to my office in about twenty-five.'

'OK, will get started on my reports first.'

Will headed to his office and started writing his report. He was about half way through when Tom came in and shut the door.

'Hey,' he sat down. 'So, what do you think he will say?'

'To be honest, Tom, I don't know,' he sat back. 'It could be literally anything, you know him, but I have a feeling it won't be good for us, anyway.'

Just then, the phone went. Will got a pen and paper and answered the phone.

'Sergeant, hope you have had a good day. Now I have been busy planning what you are to do next, so are you ready? Now, do listen carefully as I am not going to repeat these instructions.' He paused before he continued. 'At nine-thirty tomorrow morning, you are going to go, with ALL your team, minus one of course, and hold up the Westgate bank. You will not tell anyone inside the bank that you are the police, that would be too easy.'

Will stopped writing. 'You want us to commit armed robbery for you?' he questioned in disbelief.

'Yes, exactly, Sergeant. But it is not just for me, it's for your girlfriend here.'

Will sat back in his chair, he put his hand on his head. 'What are we taking?'

'All in good time, Sergeant, I will ring you on this number at nine-forty with further instructions. The security cameras are being monitored so I will be watching you from the time you enter, so no trying anything.'

'And Officer Hill...?'

'Why so formal, Sergeant? Kathy will be safe till then and I am taking such good care of her for you,' he laughed. 'But I assure you, tell anyone outside your team and she dies. They tell anyone: she dies. Fail to comply and SHE DIES.'

'Let me talk to her,' Will said insistently.

'Hello, Sergeant, don't do it. He is going to kill me, anyway,' she pleaded, scared and tearful.

'Don't talk like that, trust me. I will find you, it will be OK, just stay strong.'

'Now,' his voice came back on. 'Nine-thirty at the bank and don't be late. I will call you at nine-forty. Bye for now.' With that, he hung up.

Will put the phone down on the desk and they both looked at it in silence, not knowing what to say. Suddenly the door flew open, Tom and Will both jumped. It was Lieutenant Planter.

The Lieutenant was in his mid-forties. He was of Caribbean descent. He was five-foot-eleven with striking features. He had been on SWAT twenty years but not in New York; he transferred from Atlanta only a year ago, and he was still getting used to the way that Sergeant Falco did things. They had had many disagreements in the past and Will knew this would make things worse.

'Easy guys, just me,' said the Lieutenant. 'The Captain needs to speak with you, Sergeant, as soon as possible.'

'Yeah, sure, I will be in in a few minutes, just going over something with Hargreaves.'

'OK, but don't be too long,' He left looking very suspicious at Will and Tom as he did so.

'Shut the door again.' Will said.

As Tom shut the door, he asked, 'He really wants us to hold up a bank?'

'Yes, to make us look bad, and to save him from having to do it and risk getting arrested. We have so much on him now, he can't get caught now, can he?'

'And we are going to do this?' Tom asked, though he knew the answer, even if it's not what he wanted to hear.

'Yes, but we are going to do it our way, not his. He just doesn't know it yet. We have to talk to the team and get them in on it, but we can't do it here.' He paused, thinking. 'The diner, after shift. Everyone.'

With that, he got up and went into the Captain's office.

'You wanted me, Captain?' Will said.

'Yes, Sergeant, sit down.'

Will sat as instructed, it seemed serious.

'I have been speaking to the Captain down in internal affairs. He has removed Green from the investigation of you and your team; however, he feels that your behaviour over recent months needs looking into and so is assigning someone else. I told him that he was looking in the wrong place for the leak, to which he agreed but he said he needs to follow up what Green started, grudge or not.'

'So, what does that mean?' Will asked.

'Well, as long as you and your team are clean and you don't have any bad shoots in that period, you are good.'

'Then, we are good, Captain.'

'OK, well it's nearly end of shift, so get sorted and out of here, it's been a hell of a couple of days.'

'Yes, Captain, have we heard anything about Kathy, any clues to where she is? I mean, it's been over 24 hours.'

'Sadly not, Sergeant, they think he is holding her as an insurance policy while he pulls a job but we don't know anymore, you know he hardly leaves a trail.'

'I know, Captain, thanks.'

Will finished up and got changed before heading to the diner to meet the others.

Chapter Eleven

'Are we just waiting on Bennett? Where is he?'

'Just on the phone, Sergeant. He won't be a minute,' answered Harvey.

The diner was designed in a 60s style. There was a juke box at one end of the counter. The whole place was decorated in pink and chrome, with pictures of musicians from that era. They had gone all out to be as authentic as possible. Not usually the team's choice in an after-work drink, but it had its advantages. It was close to work and it was busy, so had plenty of ambient noise. They couldn't afford to be overheard. The waitress came over, all dressed up in a 60s outfit.

'What can I get you gents?'

'Five coffees, please,' Tom answered.

'OK, won't be a minute,' she replied.

As she went to get the drinks, she passed Bennett as he approached the table.

'So, what's going on and why the hell are we meeting here of all places?' he gestured at the surroundings while he got comfortable.

'Here we are, guys, and there's the milk and sugar. If you need a refill, just give me a shout,' the waitress said, putting everything out on the table.

'OK, thanks very much,' Will replied and waited till she was out of ear shot before he began.

***

After he explained the whole story to the team, from the kiss to the phone call, he said, 'So to get her back alive, we have to do this as a team.' He looked at them, hoping one of them would say something. There was shock and uncertainty in their faces. He didn't know which way they would go.

'And we are going to do this while on shift tomorrow? Is that right?' Palmer questioned, quite shocked at the idea of doing something that would break the law.

'Yes, we have to be there at nine-thirty,' replied Tom, seeing that the events of the last few days were all getting a bit much for Will and the exhaustion could clearly be seen on his face.

'We do this so he thinks he is getting his way, but we have ideas too. We need to be fully armed and suited up or he will get suspicious. We have to cover our SWAT badges or he will see them on camera. But we are figuring out a way to let the police know it is us inside.'

'You mean the police will be called, on us, like a real hold up; we know the drill. They could come in and shoot us, right?' asked Bennett.

'He has to believe we are following what he wants us to do. But it will be fine, they won't shoot us, and once they know it is us, they will back off and we can get Kathy back,' Will continued. 'They will be watching the bank, so we have to be careful what we do and say at all times. He won't need much of an excuse to shoot her.'

Will was tired and he wanted to go home and plan exactly what they were going to do in the morning down to the last detail. He couldn't make any mistakes this time. This man was not going to do this to him again; he should never have shown his feelings the way he did or where he did. All this was on him and so was whatever was going to happen next. He could only hope it would turn out all right.

Tom finished up 'Remember, not a word to anyone, turn up for shift as normal, we will have everything sorted out and ready. This could easily be your worst day on SWAT. So, we need complete focus and trust from all of you. Get a good sleep and we will see you in the morning.'

***

When Bennett, Palmer and Harvey had left, Tom looked over at Will, deep in thought, looking at his empty cup.

'Ready for a refill, guys?'

Tom looked up, it was the waitress with a full coffee pot in her hand. 'Thanks, that would be great,' Tom replied.

She filled the cups and walked away, serving others as she went.

'She will be OK,' Tom said as he put milk and sugar in the fresh coffees.

'Is that a question or a statement?' Will responded without looking up, with a hint of despondency in his voice.

'A statement, we will get her back safe. You just need to trust yourself and your instincts to do this.'

'Like I did yesterday, when I caused all this, you mean?' he took a sip from his coffee not looking up at Tom once.

'Will, you were not to know he would find us there, and it is not your fault. What he did yesterday and six years ago is all on him, you didn't do anything wrong.'

Will looked at him, he didn't need any reminders of that, with what had happened yesterday, he was ready to break. He had waited six years for them to be in this position and now it could all go wrong and all because he let his feelings interfere with the job. Tom could see the strain in his face.

'He wants you to snap, to mess up, he needs you to be like this,' Tom continued. 'People like him want people as good as you out of the way and he knows the ONLY way to get to you is to make it personal. He knows he can't break you any other way.'

'You are right, Tom. I know you are,' Will sat back and took a deep breath. 'I need to face up to it all at some point, and you know if we do this there will be some consequences, especially with Internal affairs crawling all over the department and waiting for us to mess up, but right now, we need to focus. We can't afford any mistakes. We were on top form today, as a team, and we need to be like that but better tomorrow.' He stood and got his things. 'Thanks for the chat. This is for the coffees.' He put fifty dollars on the table as he left.

***

Outside the diner, Palmer, Bennett and Harvey got together and were chatting.

'Harvey, you have worked with the Sergeant for a while, has he ever done anything so crazy before?' asked Bennett.

'I have worked with him for seven years, he chose me to join his team not long after he took it over. At first, he was really cool, relaxed never got mad or anything, even when things went south. Then, six years ago, we had an armed robbery at a jewellery store and it all went really bad really fast. We followed procedure and orders from the top, and the guy who has Kathy was the only one left after we took all his men down. Then he killed every hostage, he didn't have to but did. Since then, the Sergeant has been angry and obsessed with getting this guy, he has pushed himself and all us to the limit since, to make sure we don't make those kinds of mistakes again. Why do you think he is like he is? I was hoping to get this guy so the Sergeant could finally get justice and move on, but now he has Kathy, and I for one will have his back tomorrow no matter what, because he needs this. If anything happened to her after what we just heard about his feelings for her, I would hate to think what would happen. Sergeant Falco is a lethal weapon on a good day, never mind a bad one.' Harvey explained. 'So if you want to stay in this team, then get on board and fast, Sergeant needs us.'

'Well, I'm in, but why have we never been told all this?' Palmer asked.

'You really think the one who demands perfection will ever discuss the day where it wasn't good enough to save those people?'

'Good point, well just hope it all works out tomorrow then, because I have a bad feeling about this whole thing,' Bennett said.

'Me too, but we have to get on with it and do our bit, the rest can be looked at later.'

Harvey replied. 'Good night guys, get some sleep.'

***

Will rode for an hour round the streets of Manhattan, before heading home. He lived in a Park avenue penthouse, which no one at work knew, except Tom and two others. His parents had been exceptionally wealthy. His father had made his money in real estate and owned a large corporation. The building in which Will lived was also his, one of many in Manhattan. His father was Russian-American and his mother was from Brazil, an unusual combination, but Will always remembered they had been very happy, and successful. When his parents were murdered six years earlier, as an only child, Will inherited everything.

Will was never comfortable with the wealth, and as a young man had distanced himself from it. That's how he had met Tom. He had insisted on going to a regular school and he spent most of his free time with Tom and his parents. Will's parents had also looked after Tom, ensuring he and his parents had everything they needed, including health care.

When Will had joined the force, his parents had changed his last name to protect him. Their name was well known and so his real identity had never been revealed. They bought him an apartment near Tom's so people wouldn't get suspicious and any woman that came into his life, and got as far as meeting his parents, signed legal papers so they couldn't disclose anything.

It was strange living in their home now, but it was the only way he ever felt close to them. Many nights he hated being alone and so had spent them in the company of beautiful women that he had met at the parties and fundraisers he attended. He was not happy, though, and they were only interested in the money, or he became friends with them and they kept quiet about who he was. Since his parents were killed, he was scared of getting close to anyone and today was the reason why. He didn't know what he would do if something happened to the woman for whom he had dared to have real feelings.

When he got home, he sat in silence for a while before making himself some food, which he didn't eat. He showered and headed for bed. He laid there for hours, images of then and yesterday running through his mind again and again, wondering what if he had done it all differently, would they be alive? Would Kathy not have been taken? He eventually fell asleep at three a.m.

Chapter Twelve

Will's alarm went off at six-forty-five. He stirred from a deep sleep and turned it off. He came to, realising what time it was; he quickly got up and rushed round to get ready. He made himself his usual coffee, but today took it to go, as he wanted to get in early. He stopped by the front door and took a deep breath. He did a check list in his mind. He had everything he needed but he had to focus, be calm and collect his thoughts. Today he could not lose his cool, lives and jobs depended on it. He knew there was a chance that things would not go the way he had planned, that the possibility of them being arrested was high, but he had faith that they would all come through it; he doubted once the unit knew it was them, they would enter the bank. He had learned over time not to underestimate anyone, though especially those who had their mind set on causing chaos and, if necessary, death to get what they wanted. He knew today was going to be hell and he had to prepare himself for the worst, but his mind would not allow him such thoughts.

***

Will was the first to arrive, as always. He sat for a while by his locker and took his time to get ready. He sat in front of his locker when he was dressed and ready and put his head in his hands. He took a few deep breaths. As the team walked in, he stood up and got his vest out of his locker, then closed the door. The team were quiet, none of the usual banter, just brief polite conversation, but most of it was done in silence, each one mentally preparing for the day ahead.

'We all ready?' Will asked and got nodded confirmation from each of the team. 'Let's arm up. We have a bank to get to.'

He turned to them as he got to the door. 'In case I don't get a chance later, thanks for doing this, guys. I know it could cost you everything, if it should all go wrong, and I appreciate that more than you know.'

They collected their weapons from the gun cage like normal, explaining they were going training, then got in the two black SUVs and drove away.

***

Everyone kept quiet on the way to the bank, not really knowing what to say. They parked right outside the bank but so they didn't block the line of sight from inside. On his ride around last night, Will had stopped his motorbike outside the bank and had a good look around, finding the best place to park and where he knew the police would position themselves, including SWAT. They got ready in silence, preparing their uniforms so no one knew who they were. They loaded and prepared their weapons, which they were all hoping they didn't have to use, not in the bank at least.

Will knew that there was a good chance they would, in fact, get arrested and there was a good chance that he at least would lose his job. How could he tell his team that? He was so afraid that one of them would have a change of heart and then Kathy would be killed, so he felt he had only to tell them the best-case scenario. How this was going to play out, none of them knew, but it was too late to turn back.

Will got out of the cars first. People started looking. The team were fully armed and suited up but today they had nothing to identify them as police. People started moving away, knowing that something was about to happen. At nine-twenty-nine, the others got out of the cars; they looked at each other, paused and walked through the doors at exactly nine-thirty.

***

Kathy was tied to a chair at one end of what appeared to be an old aircraft hangar. She was cold and exhausted. She hadn't slept, not even when they put her on the bed that was there, but she kept thinking about what Sergeant Falco had said to her on the phone; she needed to keep hopeful. There was a desk with several television screens on it just a metre away from her and he was sat watching them intently. Apart from that, there was just a cold, dim, vast space stretching out in front of her. She could just about make out the end of the hanger in the dimness. She knew it wasn't dark, but there were no windows in the place so it was just dark and cold. She looked over at him, watching the screens. He looked at his watch then back at the screens again.

'You know you might as well kill me now, he is not going to rob that bank for you,' Kathy said defiantly.

'Well he knows better than to underestimate me.' He paused and smiled. 'And you should get to know him better, because they just walked through the door/'

'You're lying, he wouldn't,' she retorted.

'Really, am I?' He turned one of the screens so she could see it. 'He really must like you, he wouldn't put everything on the line otherwise. I have known him for a few years now and he has risked his career for two other people before; the only other people he cared about, but sadly, I had to shoot them anyway.'

'Who?' she questioned, trying to hide the fear that was building inside.

'His parents,' he said, smiling proudly.

'You are going to kill me, too, aren't you?

'That depends on him,' he replied, pointing at Will on the screen. 'If he does exactly what I say, there will be no need to hurt you, but if he doesn't, then I may have to change my mind, which is a shame. I quite like having you around.'

Kathy sat in silence, looking at the screens. She had never known Will do anything that would break the law before, he was all about the job; she was finding it hard to believe what she was seeing.

***

The Westgate bank was one of the smallest in Manhattan. It consisted of only three cashiers and two desk clerks in a moderately small room. In the far-left corner, there was a security door which Will presumed led to the vault and the manager's office. It had been bothering Will all morning. Why this bank? It was too small to hold a large amount of cash or anything that would be considered valuable, but there had to be something that he needed or he wouldn't risk getting caught, because before he took Kathy, he would have been doing this job.

The customers watched the team as they walked in. Will walked over to the first cashier and the rest stayed by the doors, pointing their weapons down away from the public.

'Where is the manager?' Will asked the woman stood behind the desk.

'He is in a meeting, do you have an appointment?' she asked in a pleasant voice and with a smile, almost oblivious to his attire and weapons.

Will hated what he had to do next. He had never drawn his weapons on any innocent person before. He took a deep breath, and looked at the security camera, knowing he would be watching.

'I do now,' he replied as he pulled his handgun and pointed it straight at her. 'Show me where he is.'

The rest of the team secured the doors and then got the staff from behind the desks and made everyone sit on the floor, backs to the cashier's desks. They still didn't point the guns directly at anyone, but made it look convincing for the cameras; he had to believe they would shoot someone, even if they had no intention of doing so.

Will followed the cashier to the manager's office. He was with a customer.

'I said I was not to be disturbed,' the manager said in a stern tone as Will and the cashier entered. Then he saw Will's gun behind her and froze, eyes wide with fear.

'I said it would be OK,' Will signalled them to get up. 'Now let's go, nice and slow, we don't want anyone doing anything stupid and getting hurt.'

He followed them out to the main part of the bank. 'You two sit down with the others, and you,' pointing to the manager, 'you go and open the vault and don't tell me you can't, I know better.'

He signalled Palmer to follow the manager. 'Tell me when you are in,' he said as they went through the security door.

It was nine-forty and the cell rang right on time.

'Yeah?' Will answered.

'Hello, Sergeant. I didn't know you had it in you, just watching here on the monitors gives me chills of excitement. I could find you a spot on my team if you want a change in career,' he laughed and then paused, almost waiting for a response before he continued. 'Now I see you have the manager opening the vault. Well done, but before you start celebrating, maybe you should take a look outside the windows. New York's finest, including you fellow SWAT members, are surrounding the building, and it appears the media has been tipped off. They know it is you and your team in there so I hope you weren't planning on an easy exit, even you will struggle with this one,' He laughed again, clearly pleased with the situation Will was now in.

'So what are we taking?' Will asked, trying to mask his anxiety.

'What's the hurry, Sergeant? Everything will be revealed in good time. I will call back when the vault is open, so I suggest you find a way to hold off the police and your friends on SWAT from coming in to get you, I would hate for you to get shot before you manage to find Kathy.' The phone went dead.

Will went over to the windows and looked through the blinds. Just as he said, there were police everywhere, including SWAT, and there were camera crews and reporters too. He scanned every building and car, making a mental note of every position each officer was in.

'Shit,' he signalled Tom over to him. 'He has gone and tipped off the media and they know it is us in here. It is going to be all over the news. There goes plan A: with the media outside watching, they are not going to let us walk out of here that easy.' Will explained quietly so as not to alert the rest of the team.

'Great, now what?' Tom asked, obviously concerned by the developing situation. 'This is going too far, Will, what if they decide to come in? What are we going to do then, shoot at our own unit?'

'We keep going. I have a plan B, but just keep it quiet for now, I don't want the others worried just yet. He was always going to try and get us in the shit; I should have realised how far he would go, though, but I got distracted with getting Kathy back.'

At that moment, the bank phone rang. They all looked over, they knew what was coming next.

Chapter Thirteen

'Hello?' Will answered the bank phone.

'Hello, this is the NYPD SWAT unit, can I speak to the person in charge, please?'

Will recognised the voice on the phone as Sergeant Holt, a trained negotiator for the SWAT unit.

'Yeah, that's me,' he replied.

'Good, now if you take a look outside, you will see that the bank is surrounded by officers. We don't want anyone to get hurt, so why don't you tell me what you want. But first, what's your name?'

'Sergeant Holt, this is Sergeant Will Falco of the New York SWAT unit Alpha team, and I want to speak to Captain Bridge. When you get him down here, he can call me on this number, but I will only talk to him, and in the meantime, I suggest you don't try anything like coming in. My team are the best trained team in the unit and we would really hate to prove that today. Get the Captain and we can talk some more.'

'Sergeant Falco, what the hell? How is it you on the other end of the phone? I can call the Captain for you and I will keep our guys out here, but you need to give me something here.'

'I wish I could, but right now I can't, not right at this moment, please just get me the Captain.'

Will hung up and looked at the others. 'That should have bought us some time, let's just hope it is enough.'

***

Captain Bridge was sat in his office, wondering where Sergeant Falco and his team were, he hadn't seen them since they arrived this morning at the start of shift. They hadn't been in the office at all, and more concerning, they had missed a call, which had never happened before; the officers in the gun cage had said they signed out their weapons for training, but they shouldn't have missed the call. It was becoming an extremely bad day. His first team had disappeared, there was a hostage situation at a bank and he still had an officer missing. He needed a coffee. He was heading over to get one when Lieutenant Planter came running over.

'Captain, you have got to see this.'

He turned on the television in the office and there it was Captain Bridges worst nightmare playing out before his eyes.

'It has been reported that the men holding up the Westgate bank just behind us here in downtown Manhattan is actually a SWAT team from the NYPD. The team leader, Sergeant Falco, and four members of his team took over the bank at nine-thirty this morning. They are holding around fifteen people hostage at this time, it is unclear what their motives are. The police outside are reluctant to move at this time but are instead trying to negotiate with them, to ensure no one gets hurt,' explained the reporter.

Captain Bridge looked at the screen in disbelief before he responded. 'What the hell is this?' he shouted, gesturing at the screen. 'Someone tell me this is some kind of joke.'

'I am afraid not, Captain' Lieutenant Planter answered. 'And now he is asking to speak to you. He says he won't talk to anyone else, what do you want me to do?'

'There has to be some reason for this,' he turned, walking towards his office. 'Get me a car out front now. I am going down there, and I will find out what is happening.'

***

The vault was finally open and, as expected, the cell phone rang.

'Sergeant, you are making an exceptional thief. Are you sure you don't want a change in career?'

'Yeah, whatever. Now tell me what the hell we are taking so we can get on with this.' His voice filled with anger and frustration at the constant tormenting, and he knew they were running out of time.

'Sergeant, that is not a very nice way to talk to me when I have Kathy here.' There was a scream of pain. 'Now be good or she will know what pain really is.'

'What the hell did you just do to her?' he responded in anger.

'Well, let's just say she has a cut on her arm. Now, you will go into the vault...'

'You bastard!' Will started pacing up and down, furious and helpless.

'Calm down, Sergeant, and listen. She can't afford for you to get this wrong. In the vault, on the right-hand side, there are some drawers. Count down five and open it, take out the contents and put them in a tube, there should be some there. Then open all the other drawers and empty all the contents onto the floor. Only you and one other member of your team in the vault, no more.'

'Then what?'

'Then you can leave as you only have one hour to get to Grand Central Station, platform three. One of my men will meet you there. When he gets the package, he will give you instructions on what to do next. Now, if all goes according to my instructions, you will get to find out where your girlfriend is. If not, she will get to meet your parents.' He hung up.

Will looked at his watch. He looked at the team and wasn't sure what was going to happen after this, he could have cost them all their jobs and if this got messed up, Kathy would be in serious danger. He knew he had to figure all this out, quick. He gestured to Palmer to join the rest of the team. 'Tom, here with me, and you get on the floor with the others,' he said to the manager.

Tom walked over to Will and they went into the back and entered the vault. The vault was small, no gold or precious items worth millions, just some cash and the drawers. The only upside was there were no cameras inside, just one that covered the door. Will opened drawer five and took out the contents.

'Blue prints?' Tom exclaimed.

'Put them in a tube and empty the other drawers out onto the floor.' Will picked one up and looked at it. 'These are valuable possession buildings. For gold and other high-priced items; there are jewellery stores, museums and all sorts here.' He looked at the ones on the floor. 'We need to somehow mark which ones we are taking, then the police can work out what he is after, there can't be many buildings he would target. With the investigation going on, he wouldn't be able to fence too much.'

'The tape from your weapons, he won't notice that missing on the cameras, as they are black and white, and no one outside the PD knows it's there, and then they will know it was us that put it there.'

'Great idea, Tom.'

Every member of Will's team had coloured tape on their weapons for identification, his was red. It had been an idea of Will's after a suspect's relative had tried to sue the unit and a member of his team when the suspect was fatally shot in a bank robbery. The team member had left because of the case and what it had done to them. His system made it impossible for anyone to know who pulled the trigger by using colours, not names on any shout, especially over the radio. And when the weapons were in the cage, they were only identified by the coloured tape, so if any were investigated for legal cases, no names were on them. Only SWAT knew whose was which colour and it was never disclosed outside the unit. The number of civil suits had been reduced to zero over the last four years; it had been so successful, each team had adopted their own system, most used numbers and letters, but Will liked to use colours.

Will took the tape off and put it on the drawer handle from where they had taken the blue prints. They walked out of the vault and the bank phone rang.

'That will be the Captain and our way out,' Will remarked.

Chapter Fourteen

'Hello?' Will answered the phone.

'Falco, is that you? This is Captain Bridge. do you want to tell me what the hell is going on?'

'Can't do that, Captain. We just want to get in our cars and leave. All the people in the bank are unharmed, and no one will get hurt, if we can just leave here.'

'You mean you want me to let you just leave with no explanation, nothing?'

'Yeah, for now, anyway. I don't want to fire at anyone out there. We are cops too, but you also know that me and my team could put down half the officers out there before they can fire one shot, which you know we don't want to do. We are fully suited for our protection, so it's going to make it difficult for your guys out there, anyway.' Will paused and took a deep breath. 'I just need you to trust me. You know me and you know I would not be doing this if I had a choice.'

'Yes, I do know you and because of that, I will let you drive away, because I know there is more to this than you can say right now. But once you have left, I can't control what happens. They will follow you and probably arrest you. Sergeant, you know Internal Affairs will be all over this and I have officers telling me you have gone too far.'

'I know, and I am very sorry for putting you in this situation, but I have to do this, and though this all seems crazy now, it will make sense soon and I will explain everything the moment I can.'

'OK, I will stand them down for you to leave, and I will see you at the station.'

Will hung up the phone and took a moment then turned to his team.

'We are good to go,' he walked over to the manager and crouched down 'I am really sorry I had to do this, please know I would never have hurt you or anyone else in this bank.'

The manager nodded at him. Will stood and headed for the doors. They came out of the bank one at a time. The street was full of squad cars and the officers were ready to fire but none of them did. There was a tense atmosphere and Will scanned everywhere, watching to see if anyone made a move. The team got into the cars they had left there earlier, all on edge, not wanting to, but ready to fire should they have to. They pulled away and drove past the Captain, who was left wondering what just happened.

'You know they are going to follow us, right?' Tom commented to Will, who was driving the first car.

'Yeah, I know. That's why, when we get there, I go in alone and find this guy, while you keep them busy as long as you can, but don't do anything stupid.'

'I thought we weren't going to get done for this? That's what you said last night, you said it would be OK and we wouldn't lose our jobs but that's bound to happen now, right?" remarked Bennett from the back.

'Yeah, sorry about that, Bennett, but if that bastard hadn't plastered it all over the news who we were, we could have avoided this,' replied Will

Tom turned round and looked at Bennett. 'The Captain will do what he can. He knows something is going on, but we can't say anything till Kathy is safe, not even if we are arrested. It will work out, don't worry,' he said, reassuringly.

Will glanced over to Tom. He was not sure that his friend was right this time; with Internal Affairs watching them, he knew his job at the very least would be on the line and he could be charged; he would protect the others as best he could but he knew that might not turn out so well. But Kathy was the one who mattered right now, she was the one with her life on the line, because his job was nothing compared to that and he would ensure his team was OK for the future.

**

They pulled up outside the station with not much time left. Will went inside with the tube while the others stood outside, ready to hold off any officers that were going to appear. As Will entered, he heard sirens approaching. He hurried to platform three. It is a big station though and he had to move fast. He got to the platform just on time and spotted the man easy; he was one of the men that had taken Kathy.

A train stopped on the platform in front of them. He stepped onto the train and took the tube from Will. As the doors were closing, he said, 'He will call YOU in an hour with a location and you had better answer the phone,' and then the doors closed.

The train was just pulling away when Will heard a voice behind him.

'Put down all your weapons and get down on the ground with your hands on your head.'

Will recognised the voice, it was Sergeant Dune from the late shift. He had never liked Will and still harboured a lot of resentment for his capabilities and the fact that he ran the sniper team, the most prestigious for any Sergeant on SWAT.

The people on the platform started backing away and watched from a distance with nervous curiosity.

'Guys, I'm not going to shoot anyone, my weapons are all safe,' Will replied as he put his rifle on the floor and turned round with his hands on his head. 'There is no need for such hostilities, you can take my weapons and I will come quietly.' Sarcasm was in his voice, covering the anxiety deep inside.

'Right, Falco. You just held up a bank and now we have to arrest you. I would say it is a pleasure, I have been waiting for the day you fell on your ass, but all this is not good for the unit, it was all over the news that one of our teams had become bank robbers, heads are going to roll over this for sure, and you will probably come up smelling of roses as always.'

'You know it,' he said smiling 'And don't put the cuffs on too tight, I have delicate wrists.'

'Very funny. Let's go. Your team are waiting for you, you know it's one thing to land yourself in the shit, but to take your team down with you is selfish, even for you.' They started walking towards the steps off the platform.

'They all went into this with their eyes open, and IF I am under arrest, should you not be reading me my rights about now or have you forgot how, while my team has been doing all the work these last few years?'

As they were walking towards the exit of the station,. Will was read his rights. When he got outside, his team were all waiting in handcuffs, Bennett and Palmer looked scared, an expression he had never seen on them before. Harvey and Tom looked as strong and defiant as always, they were so loyal; he was proud to have them on his team and hoped that one of them would take over if he was fired. Will was put into a waiting squad car as were the others. This was not part of his plan, but had a feeling this is where he wanted him, so now he had to ride with it and hope when he got back to the police station, things would get better and fast, but how could they till he got Kathy back?

Chapter Fifteen

When they got back to the station, Captain Bridge was waiting at the door and walked in with them.

'I need to talk to him alone for five minutes,' referring to Will.

'I am sorry Captain but I have instructions for them all to go straight to interview without talking to anyone,' replied the Duty Sergeant.

'Fine. Then I will go with him to the interview room and trust me, I will talk to him before any interview. As his superior, I am allowed, Sergeant.'

***

Will was sat in an interview room for ten minutes before the Captain walked in. The room was small with a square table that had a chair either side of it. Will was sat with his back to the door. He sat with his hands cuffed in front of him, not doing anything but thinking how he could get out of this mess, knowing that someone was watching through the two-way mirror to his left.

'We have five minutes, so start talking, Falco or I am not going to be able to help you,' said the Captain as he walked in the room.

'I can't tell you yet, Captain, but where is my phone, I need it?'

'Which phone, your actual phone or this one?' he asked, putting the disposable cell phone on the table in front of him.

'That one. I am expecting a call.'

'Really, well that is going to be difficult with you in cuffs, are you going to co-operate?' He sat on the edge of the desk in front of Will. 'If you don't, I can't help you or your team, just tell me what the hell is going on.'

'Look at the evidence and you will work it out, Captain. I don't know who is watching or listening, so I can't risk it.' Will was getting agitated. He knew the phone was going to ring and he needed to answer it or he could lose Kathy. 'But if I don't answer that phone when it rings, then someone will pay and it won't be me. It is going to ring in ten minutes.'

'Then I guess you have ten minutes to tell me why a highly respected SWAT officer and his team would hold up a bank, don't you, Sergeant?'

Will turned around. It was Detective Franks. He had been on the force as long as Will but chose to be a detective when Will chose to join SWAT. They knew each other quite well and had worked together on a regular basis when they started out and on the odd occasion, Will assisted in arrest warrants for Franks' department. That was the main reason Franks had asked to work on the case and be the one to question him. Franks was forty, married with two children. He was thin but stood at six-foot-three, with receding brown hair and tired eyes. He looked much older than Will and not just the two years between them. Will turned round and sat back in his chair.

'Your team aren't talking, but I guess you knew that already,' Franks continued.

'That's their choice, not mine, but I can't say anything till I have that phone call, I just can't risk it,' Will replied stubbornly.

'Well that's a problem then, I can't let you answer that cell phone till I get some answers. First you can start by telling me who the call is from you are so eager to answer,' Franks walked round the table till he was facing Will, sliding the phone till it was just out of Wills reach. Will stayed silent, staring at the phone as it moved away from him.

'We know what you took from the bank. We know what blueprints you took, thanks to you. But we still need a 'who' and a 'why'. We know that someone else is behind it. We have video footage from the bank with you on this phone several times. There is a reason for all this, of that I have no doubt but we need answers. I can't think of a reason you would do all this, knowing what was likely to happen. It's not like you, Falco. I mean, you have a temper and do things unconventionally sometimes, but break the law? There has to be something or someone forcing you to.' Detective Franks sat down and looked at Will.

'I took them for the person who is going to ring that phone, and if I don't answer it, then you are responsible for what happens, not me. Now take these damn cuffs off me!' he banged his fists on the desk, getting more frustrated as he spoke.

'Calm down Sergeant...'

'Wait a minute,' Captain Bridge interrupted, leaning on the table close to Will. 'It's him, isn't it? It has to be, that explains everything.

Falco, why didn't you come to me? I could have helped.'

'It's who? What don't I know? Does someone want to tell me what is going on?' Franks responded.

'I can't say yet,' Will insisted, looking at both of them.

The phone started to ring, they all turned to look at it. They all paused and glanced at each other. Will stood and tried to grab the phone but couldn't reach it quick enough. Detective Franks picked it up and looked at it.

'Private number, well let's just see who is calling, shall we?'

'Don't, please, I have to answer or…' Will pleaded, but before he could finish, Franks answered the phone.

'Hello?'

'Can I speak to Sergeant Falco, please?' came the voice on the other end.

'He is busy right now. Can I ask who is calling?'

'NO, Detective, you can't. Now, give Sergeant Falco the phone. NOW.'

Detective Franks looked at the phone as he handed it to Will.

'Hello?' Will said as he struggled to hold the phone with cuffs still on.

'Sergeant Falco, glad you could join me. Now, why didn't you answer the phone?'

'That would be because you made sure I got arrested and so, I am sat here handcuffed in an interview room, not telling them who you are and what is going on. They took the phone from me when we got here and so I couldn't get to it before they did. Handcuffs slow you down, a fact you will know soon enough,' said Will, clearly frustrated with everything.

'Well, thank you for getting me what I wanted. Saved me doing it, and sorry about the whole arrest thing, but I think it's quite ironic that in trying to do what's right, you break the law and get arrested. No hard feelings, but I couldn't have you following my man, now could I?' he paused. 'Well I presume you want to know where I have the wonderful Kathy?'

'Yes, where is she?' Will asked bluntly.

'She is in an abandoned building at the end of the runway at JFK. Now I would set off real soon, if you can that is. I mean, it may take a while due to your current situation, but there are a few to get through. Oh, and Sergeant, just one more small thing before you go.'

"What?' Will responded, worryingly.

'You broke our agreement, someone else answered the phone, so the lovely Kathy here has to pay the price. Good bye, Sergeant.'

Before Will could say anything, he heard a gunshot, a loud thud and a car screeching away.

Chapter Sixteen

Will put the phone on the table, sat and looked at it in disbelief. Everything he had done and he had shot her anyway. His mind went back six years. Why did he think this time, the outcome would have been different? He should have known, the man wasn't capable of doing anything that wasn't pure evil, he shouldn't have fallen for it, but this time was different for it wasn't his mistake that had caused it to happen. Will stood up and threw the chair away from him and turned towards Detective Franks.

'You!' he pointed to Franks. 'You did this. He shot her and all because you wouldn't listen to me. You had to answer the phone, be the hero!' He was angry and heading closer to him. 'Why didn't you just trust me and just listen?'

Then, suddenly, a faint voice came onto the phone. Will stopped and picked up the cell phone, he couldn't believe she was still alive.

'Sergeant, if you can hear me, please find me, I need your help.'

'Kathy, is that you? What did he do to you?'

'I'm hit in the leg, it is bleeding so much, I can't stop it,' she replied in a faint voice, obviously in great pain and very scared.

'Hold on, I'm going to come and get you, just stay awake. I am going to give the phone to the Captain, just keep talking.'

Will passed the phone to the Captain, who was still shocked by what had played out in front of him. He thought on all his years on the force, he had seen it all but this was proof that he really hadn't. Then Will turned to Detective Franks.

'I have to go and find her. She will die if you don't, take these off and let us go,' he held out his hands.

Detective Franks paused and looked at Will.

'I can get officers there in a few minutes.'

'And what if some of his crew are still there? You know we are the best to handle this' Detective Franks considered for a moment. He knew he would get into trouble for this. He had no authorisation to let them go, but he also knew it was the right thing to do. He unlocked the handcuffs and followed Will out of the interview room and down the hall to where the others were being held.

'Let them out and give them their weapons back'.

The Duty Sergeant looked at him in a questioning disbelief but didn't speak.

'Just do it, Sergeant.' Franks ordered.

All the team were released and everyone watched in amazement at how quickly and efficiently they got ready and rearmed. In a matter of minutes, they were ready to go.

'Give me the phone,' ordered Will. 'NOW!'

The Duty Sergeant passed the phone and Will dialled.

'I need two SWAT cars out front and ask Lieutenant Planter to meet us by the front doors,' He hung up and turned to his team 'Let's go and find her and finish this. Hope you got your sunglasses, guys, because the press are going to go crazy when we walk out of those doors.'

Will insisted that his team always carry sunglasses, because when the press were at an incident, the constant flashing of the cameras did nothing for their aim.

Lieutenant Planter met them at the doors. There was a quick discussion of what would happen; Captain Bridge had followed to give the go ahead to the Lieutenant, and they headed out the large doors that fronted the station. Lieutenant Planter went out first. The team put on their sunglasses and followed. As expected, the press went crazy.

'Sergeant, how are you and your team back on duty after holding up a bank?' shouted one reporter.

'What is it like to be a criminal?' shouted another.

'Attention everyone please' shouted Lieutenant Planter 'I am going to make a brief statement with regards to the incident this morning and then I will be taking your questions.'

The press frenzy gathered around Lieutenant Planter, leaving Will and his team to walk down the steps and get into the waiting cars. One news crew spotted them and followed though and held the car door, stopping them from leaving.

'How are you allowed to carry on like you did nothing? What right do you have to hold up a bank and then walk out of jail?' said the reporter. 'If that had been anyone else today, in that bank, you would have shot them, would you not?'

'No comment,' replied Will reaching for the door again. 'Now excuse me, I have work to do.'

'Work! What about those people who worked in the bank? What about them Sergeant?' she continued insistently.

'OK, I will say this as politely as I can,' he paused, putting his hand on his gun. 'Move or I will shoot you.'

She stepped back in complete shock, letting go of the door and all she could do was watch as Will closed the door and drove away.

'Did you get that?' she asked the camera crew after a moment.

'Yeah, sure did, he can't say that to people, can he?'

'No, he can't, and we are going to make sure the world knows about what kind of people are paid to supposedly protect us.'

Chapter Seventeen

'Where are we going?' Tom asked, driving the first car.

'JFK.' Will replied. 'The abandoned buildings at the end of the main runway. Bennett, radio through and get an ambulance to meet us there.'

'On it, Sergeant,' Bennett replied.

'There are several buildings down there. Any idea which one?' Tom asked.

'No. We search them all if we have to, till we find her.'

'How do you know that's where she is? You only have his say so,' Tom asked. 'And I don't trust him'

'Because if he wanted her dead, he would have shot her in the head, like he did last time. No, he wants her to live, just not be awake when we find her, which means she could have heard something.'

Wills phone rang. It was the Captain with an update on Kathy.

'Tell me,' Will answered it bluntly.

'The battery has gone on the cell. She has been shot in the leg, just above the knee. She is losing blood fast and is getting weak, but she is just holding on. You need to find her, fast.' There was obvious anxiety in his voice.

'We will, Captain' He hung up and turned to Tom 'Can't this thing go any faster?'

'Sure thing,' Tom answered as he hit the gas pedal.

***

When they got there, they stopped the cars and looked around. There was eight large buildings and time was running out. They didn't have time to check them all.

'What now?' asked Bennett 'Do we have time to check them all without back up here? That's going to take too long, isn't it?

'Wait a minute. There has to be something we are missing. Look at them, do you see anything?' Will asked.

They all looked around at the buildings, but it was bright and sunny and hard to see anything. Just then Palmer shouted, 'The one at the end, the door is slightly open, none of the others are.' They started heading towards it, when the ambulance pulled up. Will stopped.

'Wait here for the signal that we have her. We don't know if there is anyone still here,' he explained. Then ran to catch up with the others.

They got to the building with the open door. It was a disused hanger. There was a dim light coming from inside and Will spotted fresh tyres tracks outside the doors. They stopped and Will looked inside. The hanger was vast and mainly dark, with just a dim light coming from the far end, but it appeared empty. They had gone. At the far end, where the light was coming from, there was some equipment and furniture. Will scanned the dimness, then he saw her lying on the floor by a chair. All he wanted to do was get in there and get to her, but he had to follow procedure to ensure it was as empty as it seemed.

'We need to secure this place, fast,' Will said to the others. 'Tom and Bennett, you go in and to the right, Harvey and Palmer to the left, I will head for Kathy, she is on the floor at the back.'

They entered one by one following the Sergeants instructions. Will walked over slowly, watching for any signs of someone still being there. As he got close, he saw there was a lot of blood. Then he thought he saw her move, he looked to his team, who confirmed it was all clear.

'Get that ambulance in here!' he signalled to Palmer, who had started back towards the door in search of lights. Will knelt by her to see if she was still alive, so scared he might be too late. His heart was racing. He had been here before, but this time, he was praying for a different outcome. He couldn't handle that kind of emotional pain again. It had nearly destroyed him last time around.

'Kathy, can you hear me? Please, answer me.'

There was fear in his voice and he could feel the tears building up.

'Sergeant,' she spoke so softly he could hardly hear her. 'The new diamond store.'

He put his head closer 'What?'

'The new diamond store. That is what he is after and he is going there tonight. Go and get him for me?' She was barely conscious now. Will sat on the floor and rested her head on him holding her hand, waiting for the ambulance to come in.

'We will, sweetheart, we will. Now you rest, the ambulance is here and you are going to be just fine, I promise.' Relief flowed over him. This time, he had got there in time.

***

After the ambulance left, Will called Captain Bridge.

'She is alive, well, just, anyway,' he paused taking a deep breath. Now was not the time for all his built-up emotions to come out. 'Can we get two armed officers to the hospital, at least till we get him?'

'They are on their way now,' replied the Captain.

'Can we get someone to look through the blueprints that were taken, and check if one is a diamond store? Something Kathy said to me, it could be a new business, so can we check for that too?'

'I will get them on it and tell them to call you with an address.'

Will closed the phone and looked at Tom.

'We need to secure this place for evidence to nail this guy,' Will said as they started heading for the door.

'The guys have done it already. There are four squad cars just arrived, as well as CSI, they will take over now. We can leave when you are ready. She will be OK, now we just have to go and get him.'

Chapter Eighteen

As they were heading towards the cars, Will's phone rang. It hadn't taken long to find the store. New diamond stores didn't open up very often, even in Manhattan. Will knew most of them with all his years on SWAT; someone had tried to rob the majority of them at some point.

'What's the address?' he questioned. 'OK, call the store, tell them we are en-route. Don't broadcast anything on the radio, he could have a scanner. Phone Detective Franks and get him to meet us there.' He hung up.

'Where is it?' asked Tom.

'Broadway,' replied Will. 'I know the place, I got some earrings from there last month.'

'Not saying a word to that, man,' Tom commented, smiling.

'Yeah, that would be good right now.' Will replied.

***

They parked away from the store, their large black SUVs didn't exactly blend into normal traffic, and he would spot them before he got close. They walked down the street, watching carefully as they went, trying to hide amongst the crowds that were rushing about. Will knew there was a chance that he may already be watching the store. He had often, over the years, watched from somewhere close while his team pulled a job, or before they went in so they knew the police didn't know his plans. Luckily, today, he wasn't.

Detective Franks was already inside. He had started to brief the staff and was waiting for Will to arrive, to finish that as he only knew part of the facts.

'It seems his aim is to come after you are closed. He knows you have a top-quality security system in place, which is why he had the blueprints stolen. He also wants to fly under the radar on this because I think it could be his last job as we are getting close; now, I need to have a good look around,' Will said to the manager. 'And don't leave anything out. The rest of you,' he said to his team, 'stay in the back, we can't afford to be seen.'

The store was quite large, three walls covered with glass display cabinets, in front of which were three counters with glass tops and fronts. The windows had no displays and had metal shutters on the outside for security when the store was closed. There were three back rooms, a small staff room with kitchen with no security, the manager's office and safe room where the most valuable pieces were kept; both rooms were secure and had cameras. Will knew the best way in was through the staff room so would prepare his team for that option. After the tour, he went back to where the team were waiting.

'Right, here is what we do. Franks, you are going to leave with a bag like a customer. He is going to be watching this place any time soon. You will go to the bar opposite and sit in the window. My team are going to stay inside, back here till closing, then behind the side counters. The staff and manager will leave and lock up as normal. The manager will come and join you in the bar, Detective. We need him later to reopen the door and lock up when we are finished.'

'Do we know what time they are coming?' Harvey asked.

'No, sadly. Kathy only overheard it was tonight. We could be here for a while, so one of the staff will go out and get us some water and maybe even some biscuits.' He allowed himself a smile. 'When he does show, we put the lights on. That's your signal to come in, Detective, with some officers and arrest them.'

'Where will they be positioned?' asked Franks.

'A few streets away. When you get to the bar, phone for what you need. NO radios and speak with an officer you trust; we know this guy has someone in the PD on pay roll and I don't want this to be screwed up.' He took a deep breath. 'Any questions? Because now is the time to ask.'

'Are you sure he will be here and not just leave it to his men?' Bennett asked. 'Because after today, I really want to get this bastard.'

'Don't we all, but I am very sure he will as this is a big job and he thinks we are still looking for Kathy and trying to figure it all out. He doesn't know we know what he is after, so to him, he is safe, and that to him is as good as an invitation. He hates the fact he has had to sit on the side-lines for so long and just watch as his men pulled jobs and often screwed up. If this is his last big score, he won't want to miss it.'

'How many men will he have with him?' Tom queried

'Don't know. His known jobs have had between five and ten men,' Will replied.

'Have you heard how Kathy is yet?' Tom responded.

'No,' Will hesitated and looked at his phone. 'Waiting for the call, she has armed officers with her, and we will be kept up to date if anything happens.'

***

The store was closed and the team were sat in the dark. It was getting late and nothing was happening. Tom was sitting next to Will behind the right-side counter.

'So, what's going to happen now?' Tom asked quietly.

'With what?' Will reacted harshly, frustrated and tired by the whole day and now the long wait.

'With you and Kathy.'

'What do you mean? Nothing. Nothing can happen,' Will said insistently.

'Will, it is not like before all this happened. Everyone knows now, even the Captain. You can't exactly ignore it all, can you?'

'No, but we can move on from it and still work together. Tom, you know nothing can happen while we are on the same team. No matter how I feel about her, we will find a way to get past it.'

'But can't she change teams or something? I mean, after all this, it is obvious there is something worth pursuing.'

'I won't force her to do that, it's not fair. It could jeopardise her future in the unit and there is no way that the Captain would let me take over another team.'

'Well, I think you need to discuss it with her at the very least, when this is all over. I mean, I would say she feels the same for you as you do for her.'

'What makes you say that?' Will turned to face Tom, curious by his comment.

'The way she looks at you whenever she gets the chance, and the fact she never slapped you when you kissed her,' he said, smiling.

'Right, Tom, that's your opinion, and maybe if she had slapped me, none of this would have happened.'

'Has a woman ever slapped you for kissing her?' Tom asked.

'No. Why?'

'Just wondered,' Tom laughed, then looked at Will and changed his tone. 'You know you will find someone who will like you for who you are and not just what you got. Right, man?'

'Yeah, and maybe one day she will just walk into my life,' Will said dismissively.

'Maybe she already has.'

Just then, a noise came from one of the back rooms.

'It's them, get ready.' Will whispered to Tom and signalled to the others behind the opposite counter. Torch lights came into the store from the back, six in all. Then the lights suddenly came on.

'Freeze, don't move or I will shoot you. You are all under arrest,' Will ordered.

Chapter Nineteen

'Put your hands on your head and lay face down on the floor,' Will ordered.

'Well, Sergeant, it seems I underestimated you this time, doesn't it?' he replied as he got down on the floor.

'Yeah, you could say that now, couldn't you'

'How did you work it out so fast? That is unusual for the NYPD because normally, I have done a job, escaped and it takes them days to figure out it was even me.'

'Well, Kathy helped with that one. It seems you underestimated her, too.' Will answered as he went over to him.

'She managed to hold on, did she? Well she is good, can really see what you like about her, perhaps the leg was the wrong place to put the bullet, next time I will have to change that.' He paused for a moment 'Well I think I will stay quiet now, till I speak to my lawyer.'

Will stood over him, crouched down and put a gun to his head.

'Go on, Sergeant, shoot me'

'Will, what are you doing? Put it down, you don't have to do this, we have him now.' Tom said as he went over to him.

Will went to pull the trigger, and paused, his heart was saying 'do it pull the trigger, kill him it's what he deserves.'

'WILL!' Tom reacted.

Will put the gun down and Tom breathed a sigh of relief.

'They wouldn't want me to, I joined the force to do what's right and my parents and Kathy feel the same, and it will give me more satisfaction to see you behind bars for the rest of your life, you bastard.' Will stepped back putting his gun away.

Just then, Detective Franks and fifteen officers came in and took the six men into custody.

'Sorry I ever doubted you, Sergeant, I should have known better, and I am really sorry I got one of yours shot, too.'

'It's all right,' Will said putting his hand on Detective Franks shoulder. 'We have him now and I reckon he would have used any excuse to shoot her. He didn't want her spoiling his plan, but he never realised how strong she is.'

'Well, I hope she is OK.'

'Thanks, all right guys, let's go' Will said as he left the store with a satisfactory smile on his face.

***

All Will wanted to do now was write his report and get to the hospital to see how Kathy was doing. He was exhausted, as were the rest of the team. These last three days had been hell for all of them. Will got a coffee and was heading towards his office when he saw three detectives walk in and head for the Captain's office. He went into his office, sat down in his chair and was about to close the door when he heard the Captain shout.

'Falco, get in here!'

'What now?' he thought. He got up and went next door.

'Yes, Captain?' he said as he walked in. 'I was just going to write up and get to the hospital.'

'No, you are not, Sergeant, you have to go downstairs with these detectives.'

'What the hell for?' Will said angrily. He was not in the mood to be messed about now.

'There is still the matter of the bank hold up to sort out and now we have a reporter saying that you threatened her life.'

'You have got to be kidding me. Can this not wait till the morning?' Will was getting angry, he had had enough for one day.

'No, it can't wait, and I wish it was a joke, but apparently she has you on tape, saying you will shoot her.'

'Shit!' Will hit the filing cabinet next to him. 'Captain, it was a slip of the tongue, I just wanted her out of my way. We were on our way to find Hill and…'

'Well, now Sergeant, you have to go and explain it to these detectives downstairs, because that reporter has filed a complaint with them.' He stood and walked over to Will. 'Listen, I know you have had a shit couple of days and all you want to do is go to the hospital and be with Kathy. But now you have to go and sort this mess out and no more 'no comment' bullshit like earlier. That's if you want to keep your job. I just hope this has not gone too far.'

'Am I being arrested for something? Do I need a lawyer or my rep?' Will asked.

'No, not yet anyway, and I have managed to keep your team out of it, being as it was only you that made the threat. This is serious, I won't lie to you. So, co-operate and we will try and sort this.'

'Thanks, Captain. Do we know how Kathy is yet?'

'They said she lost a lot of blood, but you found her just in time. She had surgery to remove the bullet and repair some of the damage. She is going to be fine, just off work for a while,' the Captain explained. 'You did the right thing, but you went about things in the wrong way.'

Will reluctantly agreed to go downstairs. As they were walking across the office, Tom came over to Will.

'Sergeant, what's going on?'

'They just need me to go and answer some questions about today. Do me a favour and go and sit with Kathy till I get there?'

'Yeah, sure, no worries. I was going to pop in anyway. I will see you there soon?'

'I hope so, I really do.' Will replied as he exited the office with the three detectives.

Chapter Twenty

Will had been sat in the interview room for two hours, the same room he had been in earlier in the day. He had answered questions about the bank ten times over and had just answered one question about the reporter incident. He was tired and frustrated. He should have been at the hospital hours ago, not stuck here. He was pacing up and down in an attempt to stay calm but the trouble was, it wasn't really working. They had decided that no further action would be taken over the hold up and the matter was now closed, due to the circumstances in which it was undertaken, and they had discovered who it was that had been tipping him off. It had all been arranged, that Will would be working the witness move, and it had been the same detective that had tipped off the press to his name and details. He remembered him, as he had been one of the detectives in the park, he had been the inside man through the last few years. Will felt better as he now knew the whole story.

Now though, there was still the stupid comment he had made to that reporter in the heat of the moment, and something told him he wasn't going to get away with that so lightly; the press didn't always paint his unit in a good light, made out that suspects were victims and he had been a target on a regular basis, but they had never got something like this on him before. He was more angry with himself, than he was with them or even her; he knew better than to let his emotions interfere but these past few days that was all he had done and he just wanted it all to be over, whatever the cost.

The door opened and Captain Bridge and two of the detectives came in.

'Sergeant, we have been in talks with the TV station and the reporter,' the Captain started.

'So, what's the situation now?' Will sat down. Captain Bridge sat opposite as the detectives stood behind him by the door.

'They are prepared to drop the charges and not show the tape and destroy it on three conditions,' Captain Bridge continued.

'Why do I reckon I am not going to like these conditions?' Will responded with a tone of sarcasm in his voice.

'You don't have to like them, Sergeant, you just have to do them.'

'And if I refuse?' Will queried.

'You will be charged for threatening her life and lose your job, so I would say you are going to do this.'

There was a pause. Will stood and walked to the two-way mirror. Without turning around, he asked, 'So what are these conditions?'

'First, an apology in person to the reporter and her camera man. Second, you will be required to pay a $100,000 fine, which will be donated to charity. You can pay it over time if you need to'

'Well the money is easy enough if they accept cheques. The apology, I think I can manage. So, what's the third?'

'You are not going to like this bit, but you have to give a press conference on the events of the last three days, leaving out the personal details which got you into this of course, though I am sure the press would love those bits. We don't want that on the front page. It will be the day after tomorrow.'

'You are joking, right? Me give a press conference? You know that is not going to go well.' Will turned and looked at the Captain.

'Yes, you, and a message from the Chief. You have got to be nice and polite, no swearing, shouting or signs of aggression in any way. We have some damage control to do with the public and media after all this, and being as you are responsible for that, you are going to front it. You mess this up and...'

'And what?' Will responded sternly, arms folded.

'You lose your team.'

'Lose my team? As in, no longer have one? Or as in, I get a crap heap of a team?'

'As in no longer have one. You will be off SWAT and on traffic duties for the rest of your time in the force. Sorry, Sergeant, this was the best I could do.'

Will shook his head. He had done this, and he didn't have the best record of staying out of the Captain's office. This time, he had to pay the price.

'Yeah. I know, this is my mess so I guess I have to be the one to clean it up. I am not sure why you keep me sometimes, Captain, I am more trouble than I am worth.'

'Sometimes,' said the Captain as he got up and they walked to the door. 'But life would be dull without you around and you know you are the best I got.' He smiled. 'Now get to the hospital. You can finish your reports next shift in. I am going home to my wife, and Sergeant, you did all this to save her, don't throw away how you feel for a job, you will regret it.'

As they left, the two detectives hung back for a moment.

'What the fuck? How can a cop afford that much money?'

'I don't know, man, but I do know if that had been anyone else, they would have been off the force, for sure. Maybe we should do a little detective work into Sergeant Falco'

***

Will packed up, got changed and headed for the hospital. He had so much going round in his head. His parents and how he lost them, and now the woman he was falling for had almost died at the hands of the same man. People kept telling him what the Captain had said, that he was the best, but how could he be? The last six years, he had been fighting inside and out, he knew that he had been so angry; at friends, Tom had seen him through most of it and his work had become so much of a focus. He wanted the guy so bad that he couldn't see that he was been set up till it was too late, and that emotional attachment to it all scared him. He had also thought that when the man who killed his parents was caught, it would be all right and he would find some peace. He now though he just felt empty inside and guilty. The events of the last three days had all happened because of him and now he didn't know what to say or do to make it right. He just knew what he had to do now.

When he arrived at the hospital, he headed for the front desk.

'I am looking for Officer Kathy Hill.'

'Yes, let me check for you,' The receptionist looked on the computer. 'Third floor, room twenty-one.'

'Thanks very much.' Will smiled and headed for the elevators. In the elevator, he tried to figure out just what he was going to say to Kathy, with the Captain's last words going round in his head. He got out and walked down the hall, looking for room twenty-one. He got there, he acknowledged the police officer still on guard at her door. Tom was still sat with her, as promised. When he saw Will, he came over to the door.

'Hey man, how are you doing? What happened with the detectives?'

'I'm OK, just some crap over that reporter at the car. She really wanted my blood. I have to apologise, pay her $100,000 and do a press conference, at which I have to be nice and polite or I am off the unit.' He tried to laugh it off but inside he was furious, mainly with himself.

'That is bullshit, with everything that was going on at the time, how could they try and do you for that?'

'I know, but she got it on tape so I have no choice, it was either that or work traffic for the next twenty years or so. How is she, anyway? He asked, gesturing towards Kathy.

'She is all right, I guess. She lost a lot of blood and had surgery to remove the bullet. She is in a hell of a lot of pain as you would expect, but she will be fine. She was asking for you before she went to sleep,' he paused and looked at Will, whose eyes were fixed on Kathy. 'Listen, I best go or Lynne is going to kill me. See you tomorrow?'

'Yeah, sure thing. I'll be in. Night.'

Tom got his things and left. Will walked across the room. It was a private room with large windows covered by the closed blinds, all kinds of monitors and tubes everywhere. She looked so peaceful lying there asleep, even after all she had been through. He bent over and kissed her on the head and sat in the chair next to the bed.

Five minutes later, he was asleep.

Chapter Twenty-One

It was morning when Kathy woke, she moved and cringed with pain. She looked around. There he was, next to her, asleep. She smiled. She wasn't sure what was going to happen now, they hadn't had chance to speak about the kiss or what would happen now; she knew what she wanted but he had jumped away so fast, she wasn't sure what he would say or do. It all depended on what the Captain chose to do about the new team and if, in fact, she had passed her exams.

A nurse came in. She opened the blinds and the sunlight poured in. Kathy smiled at the warmth of it, then turned to the nurse.

'Has he been here all night?'

'Since about three, I believe,' the nurse replied as she was checking the monitors and drips, and then her dressings.

'Can you do me a favour, please?' Kathy asked her.

'Of course, what can I do?'

'Bring him a coffee with milk and four sugars.'

'Four sugars?' the nurse reacted in shock.

'Yeah, four, thanks very much.' she smiled.

Kathy lay there watching him sleep till the nurse came back with his coffee. She wondered for a few moments what he had been through these last few days; she wasn't sure what was going to happen with the fact he robbed a bank either but she was happy he was sat there at that moment.

'Here we are,' she smiled as she put the coffee down next to Will. 'The doctor will be in soon to talk to you and check your leg'

'Thanks,' replied Kathy.

As the nurse left, Kathy reached for Will's hand and shook it gently.

'Sergeant. Hey, Sergeant, time to wake up.'

He slowly opened his eyes, then sat up, quickly when he realised exactly where he was, then he smiled when he saw her.

'Morning, Sergeant, did you sleep well?'

'Not really, how are you doing now?' he asked, standing up and moving to release the stiffness from sleeping in a chair.

'Right now, I could scream with pain.' Her eyes following him as he moved around the room. 'But I am OK. The doctor will be in soon, so I will know more then. They said you got to me just in time, so thank you for that and Tom told me you caught him so thanks for that as well.'

'Are you kidding? It was my fault you ended up like this, and I am glad you were still awake to make sure we got him. He won't be hurting anyone else for a very long time. What time is it?' Will asked while looking round for a clock.

'Around eight, there's a coffee there for you,' she smiled.

'Thanks,' he smiled back and walked towards the window. 'I have to get going in a minute, I am on shift today.'

'No, you are not, Sergeant,' came a voice from the door. 'You and your team have the day off; your shift is covered.'

'Hi, Captain.'

'Morning, Hill, how are you?' Captain Bridge asked as he walked into the room and sat in the chair where Will had spent the night.

'Not great, but I'll be fine,' she smiled, putting on a brave front.

'Sergeant, you look like crap, go home get a shower and a couple of hours. I don't want to see you till at least twelve, I will sit here till then.'

'But Captain—' Will responded.

'No buts, Falco. Go home.'

Will finished his coffee, got his stuff and headed for the door. He knew he wasn't going to get his way, so he thought he might as well head home for a sleep. He turned to Kathy. 'See you later.'

***

He went home, he had something to eat and then got a shower. As the water flowed over him, he felt relief. Kathy was going to be all right, he knew it would take time for her to be back on duty and he would be short for a few months, but that would not be a problem as she was coming back. He still hadn't decided what he was going to do now; he had crossed a line with that kiss. Maybe he should talk it over with Kathy and see what she wanted. Tom was right, they couldn't ignore what had happened, and maybe deep down he didn't want to. But for now, he would play it by ear and see what happened. After his shower, he laid down. Within minutes, he was asleep.

At one p.m., he woke, feeling better than he had in days, so relaxed. He looked at the clock and jumped out of bed. He should have been back at the hospital by now. He paused. He knew she would have had plenty of people visiting though, she was popular through the whole department. He got ready and had decided he would wait for her to talk about what had happened; it was better than him presuming what she wanted. He couldn't even begin to guess what it would be now.

***

There was no longer an officer on her door, so he walked straight into her room. Gina was sat with her; they were chatting and laughing, it was a wonderful thing to hear, Will thought. Gina worked in SWAT dispatch and had done for ten years. She was responsible for taking all SWAT calls into the unit via phone or radio and paging or radioing the appropriate team, so on a day to day basis, she was often in contact with Will. The New York SWAT unit had designated teams, and Gina had to sort all the calls; they had their own dispatch unit, to make it much easier on the PD dispatch, especially on busier days, though there was only a handful of people that worked with Gina. She was dedicated to her work and loved the job. She was also probably one of the best at it too; she avoided sending Will to jobs that another team could handle and only called when Will's and his team's expertise and skills were needed. She got on with everyone and was always the life and soul of any party. She was only five feet tall, but made up for it with her bubbly personality. She was thirty-five and her mother was of Caribbean descent. She had had a bit of a fling with Will when she had only been on the unit a few months. They were now good friends and she knew his past and wanted the best for his future. She was better friends with Kathy, though. They had hit it off when Kathy came to New York three years earlier, but she still kept Will's secrets; a fact he appreciated.

'OK, if you don't need anything else, I'm going to get going,' She winked at Kathy as she stood, then smiled before she turned and headed to the door. 'I can see you are in safe hands. See you later.' She said, smiling at Will as she left.

'Thought you were coming back at twelve?' Kathy commented, looking at the clock on her night stand and smiling 'Never known you to be late before.'

'Yeah, sorry, I was asleep. What did the doctors say?' he asked while walking towards the bed.

'It's OK. You look better than you did this morning anyway, and I had plenty of company. After the Captain, Bennett and Palmer came, then Gina, as you saw.'

'Great, at least you weren't bored, so are you going to tell me what the doctor said?' Will asked as he sat in the chair next to her. He had an underlying need to know for sure she was going to be OK.

'Yeah. They said I need to stay in for a couple of days, to make sure I am healing right. I have to use those for a couple of weeks too,' she pointed to a pair of crutches across the room. 'I am also going to need some physio to get the muscle working properly again.'

'So when will you be back at work? Did they say? I mean, I don't mind being down a team member but I don't like the thought of that long term.'

'Well, I sort of need to talk to you about that one,' she said as she moved uncomfortably.

'Why? Did they say you can't come back to active duty or something? I mean, they can't expect you just to sit behind a desk,' Will reacted, concerned. He couldn't imagine work without her now.

'No, of course not, takes more than a gunshot wound to stop me, but I have some good news and some bad news for you; at least, they are both good for me.' She paused and looked at Will. 'The Captain told me earlier that I passed my Sergeant's exam.'

'Wow,' He was surprised. 'That's great but you never said anything.'

'No, I know, but I wasn't really sure how it would all go,' she paused 'And it means I am leaving the team.'

'What do you mean, leaving? You can still be on the team as a Sergeant, you can be number two. I know Tom wouldn't mind.'

'Well actually there are two reasons I can't stay on the team. First, because they have asked me to lead the new team, as part of the expansion. It is a great opportunity for me. They want me to pick and train five new SWAT members to work alongside you on days, it will take a couple of months to get them ready, but the Captain believes I am ready for this, which is great. The second reason I am leaving, though, is because of you…'

Will looked shocked. 'I don't understand. I mean, if it is because of all this, then…'

'No, it's not that. Getting shot is a risk of the job, I know that, but I spoke to the Captain and we agree, it wouldn't be appropriate…'

'I told the Captain that nothing else would happen and…'

'Sergeant, would you let me finish?'

She sat up a little and smiled. 'Don't you see, I want something else to happen. We agreed it wouldn't be appropriate if we were to be in a relationship. That is, of course, if that's what you want.' She looked at him and waited for a reaction.

'Right,' he paused. 'I don't know what to say. I was going to talk about it at some point, of course, but I didn't know that's what you wanted, especially after all this happened.'

'Will, I don't blame you for what happened and I have been wanting something to happen for months, but thought you weren't interested, but now I know you are, it changes things. So, come here.'

She took his hand as he stood and guided him to the bed. He sat on the bed and kissed her; it was perfect this time, with no regrets, no guns, just them.

He sat on the bed and looked at her. She was so beautiful, and he had everything he ever wanted. Someone that liked him for him. Someone who he trusted and could really begin to see a future with. He wasn't sure though how he would tell her everything: the truth about who he was and about his parents. He wasn't sure he should tell her until he knew where this was all going. How, though, could he have a relationship based on a lie? Because she was bound to discover the truth in the end.